Seven Sisters Down Under

Margaret Sherlock

Seven Sisters Down Under

Shorelines  Publishing

First published 2008 by

Shorelines Publishing
3 St. Mark's Drive, Meadfoot, Torquay,
Devon. TQ1 2EJ

Copyright © 2008 Margaret Sherlock
ISBN: 978-0-9559710-0-6

Cover artwork by
Invertcreations@blueyonder.co.uk
Printed by Short Run Press Limited, Exeter, Devon.

Dedicated to Penny
Always remembered, always loved

Thanks to:

My six sisters, who hopefully after reading this book are still speaking to me, I love you all from the bottom of my heart.

Emma, whose encouragement after reading the first scribbled, long-hand draft, gave me enough confidence to embark on the steep learning curve that followed.

Barry, for buying me my first computer, even though he is convinced that their creation was the work of the devil – keeping a safe distance from it at all times!

Niki, for introducing me to the complexities of the computer and her endless patience in the face of my complete ignorance.

Lil, for the time given in providing her expertise, needed for type-setting and bringing the whole process together.

Linda Haddrell, for editing the final draft and Tracey Turner for transforming my *scrappy bits of design* for the cover, into a professional piece of artwork.

A tip from nature:
Your ears are not made to shut;
your mouth is

Seven Sisters Down Under

1

The loud thud, followed by an eerie sound of scraping, overwhelmingly intruded on my already fitful sleep; dragging my consciousness up into the dark reality of the shack. I fumbled frantically for what seemed like an age to switch on the bedside lamp, and the stark glare of its light prevented me from seeing for several seconds, before the soft moaning of someone in pain galvanized me into leaping out of bed. The moaning came again, and now fully awake and able to see, I headed towards the anguished noise; knowing it was Alice.

It had been Alice's turn in the middle bunk bed, and waking at two a.m. to go for a pee, she had misjudged the height of the bunk to the floor. Disorientated with sleep, her legs had slid forth into nothingness – whacking her knees, shoulder and face on the bunks heavy framework – as she'd floundered for solid ground. The short stature of her body, and the extra weight she carried on it, had stacked the odds against her surviving the fall without damage.

She was not a pretty sight, huddled on the floor bleeding and confused, and I knew by the clear light of morning, the damage – especially to her face – would look even worse. Her eyes, wide with shock and already swollen from the impact, reminded me of a wounded animal that had been cornered and was now waiting for the final blow to end its frightened life.

I now felt wide awake, even though there were still several hours before daybreak. After making her comfortable and reassuring myself that none of her injuries was life-threatening, we both climbed wearily into the double bed, preferring the comfort and confinement of sheets, to sitting

1

around in the dimly lit confines of the cramped wooden building.

Unable to succumb to the protective veil of sleep, my mind ran over the events of the previous day – the **13**[th]. It had been a bad day from start to finish, and now finally Alice's painful intrusion on my much needed sleep made me wonder (not for the first time) if the effort of this trip had been worth it.

Although this is our third full day in Australia, we are all still locked in the effects of jetlag – wide awake in the early hours of the morning and functioning like the walking dead during the day. It was naive (especially on my part) not to have calculated this 'non- time' into the equation. The months of excited planning, the weeks of choosing clothes and cosmetics that didn't eat too much into our hard-earned savings, and then the arduous travelling from one side of the world to the other – for what? We still haven't been able to capture the 'I'm on holiday' feeling. And jetlag aside, the main reason for this lack of expected joy, is the accommodation. We have unwittingly committed ourselves to spending the first ten days of our 'trip of a lifetime' in a large shed.

There are six of us – all sisters – crammed into two of these large sheds (or shacks as they've become not-so affectionately named). Our seventh sister Lilian – who lives here in Sydney, and is no doubt sleeping very peacefully in her comfortable home at leafy Lugarno – had arranged our accommodation for the first ten days of our three-week trip. To be fair, we had mentioned to her several times that our budget for accommodation was tight, and she had warned us that it was school holidays and good deals would be hard to find. Plus, to be even fairer, the six of us had all agreed, after seeing the paperwork that Lilian had taken the trouble to send us, that this area was ideal for the beach and shops. But the reality of our situation, and the discomforts we would have to face, became apparent the minute we unlocked the doors of the two large sheds – advertised as 'Deluxe Cabins'.

This particular shed was shared by the three oldest sisters. The reasoning behind this decision being older means quieter, therefore less intrusive on each other. Alice, being the oldest at sixty-five, should theoretically be the quietest and most sensible, but after her latest attempt to get to the loo, I was beginning to wonder. Even now, having fallen into a restless sleep, her loud vibrating snores – just inches from my ear – have given me a head full of painful throbs. Moving closer to the edge of the bed and pulling the top cover over my ears doesn't help much. Sleep has abandoned me to reality, so my irritated thoughts move on from Alice, and her noisy slumber.

Sally, the second eldest at sixty-two, is asleep in the bottom bunk. The snoring noises coming from the small anti-room that houses the bunks, are not as loud as Alice's night noises, but they're loud enough and the little snorts and snuffles at the end of each snore are particularly irritating. Fortunately these sounds are now slightly deadened by the fully closed sliding door that separates the anti-room. Before tonight, no one had bothered to slide it across into the closed position, but now, sound insulation is my number one priority.

For the last three days – and I've no reason to doubt for the next seven – our greatest desire has been to sleep in the double bed. The sleeping facilities of each shed consist of one double bed and three bunk beds. The double bed, made up with crisp, white linen, is typically comfortable and spacious (when sleeping alone) and is particularly inviting when you've spent two days travelling without any sleep.

The bunk beds, on the other hand, are small, vinyl covered mats, set within a three-tiered, strong wooden framework which is bolted to the wall. The top bunk – accessible by a thin, metal ladder, anchored from floor to ceiling down one side of the whole set-up – was dismissed as a possible sleeping area from day one. For starters, while mounting the thin metal rungs of the ladder, it soon became obvious that unless the soles of your feet were as tough as leather, you needed to be wearing shoes – and we weren't too happy to keep these under our pillow. After worrying visions of trying to manipulate my way down in the middle of the night, in bare feet, I felt it prudent to have a dummy run in daylight. After first banging my head on the ceiling while arranging to go forward, then turning to go backwards, I found the cutting bars of the ladder made me scream with pain! I declared (in foul language) the uselessness of this space. After witnessing my contortions Alice and Sally agreed and promptly started using it as a much needed, new storage space.

The middle bunk, being the one most favoured of the remaining two, (though obviously not for Alice, after her speedy exit from it earlier) was the easiest to climb into. The bottom bunk, being down on floor level, was dark and claustrophobic, easily accessible to creepy crawlies, and very awkward to get into unless your back had maintained the agility of youth.

Another disadvantage to sleeping in either bunk was the lack of proper bedding. We could have hired this at an extra cost, but because of our aforementioned tight budget, Lilian very kindly sorted out some of her own bedding – sleeping bags and liners.

4

Sleeping bags and their liners are made from slippery nylon material. Couple this with the smoothness of vinyl mats, and you don't need much of an imagination to visualise the difficulties of manoeuvring into a comfortable position for sleep. So from day one we decided to be democratic and take nightly turns in using the precious double bed.

Alice being the eldest, claimed first turn. Sally grabbed the middle bunk, leaving me the floor bunk, with night creatures for company. Second night, Sally, feeling very superior, enjoyed her night in the coveted bed. I moved up in height and status to the middle bunk after helping to roll Alice into the bottom one.

At last, it's my first turn in the privileged space. Even though the plans for the day had gone horribly wrong, my anticipation of the double bed and what it promised, had kept me smiling. Now, I find myself not only obliged to share the bed, but denied the much needed sleep I felt sure I'd catch up on.

Glancing for the umpteenth time at the illuminated clock on the small cooker brings a sigh of despair – 4.32 a.m. and I'm not even sleepy. Envy mingles with resentment as I'm forced to listen to the noisy sleep of my sisters. I remember feeling outraged when Sally had said the night before, 'You snore as well, Margaret,' and then a little superior when she'd added, 'but in a softer, quieter tone, similar to your voice.' Well right now I wouldn't care if I snored loud enough to bring the house down and my voice changed to that of a fish wife, if only I could get some sleep.

The idea of this Australian trip was given the first flicker of life when Lilian and George sent Sally sufficient funds to visit them for a few weeks. This act of generosity was their way of helping a member of the family to deal with tragedy.

A year ago Sally sadly lost her only daughter – the youngest of her four children – to breast cancer. Penny was loved by everyone and is still deeply missed. One of her many attributes was being in the front line for trying anything new, especially when it came to travel. Six months after Penny's untimely death, Sally felt able to take advantage of Lilian and George's offer, but wasn't adventurous enough to make the trip alone.

June, a younger sister who, like me, had left home in her late teens to work in Jersey – and has lived there ever since – had been longing to visit Lilian and George's adopted land; and here was the perfect opportunity.

Before long, the topical conversation of Australia, that had rippled through the family, gathered momentum and seized the imagination of several more souls hungry for adventure. In the blink of an eye (or so it seems now) and before we had time to think about whether we could really afford it, six sisters had been irrevocably booked on the long haul flight.

Allowing us six months to save and prepare, the decided date of departure was 9th April 2005; leaving Heathrow at 10.30 p.m., a good time to depart we were told, ensuring plenty of sleep. A forty-five minute stop at Hong Kong airport would be the only interruption to our journey, before flying on to Sydney and three whole weeks of glorious, relaxing sunshine.

To keep the record straight, I should state here and now that I also have six brothers. A couple of them showed interest in wanting to join us. But afraid that the whole set-up was getting out of hand, it was agreed, at least by us girls, that neither men nor children would be allowed on this trip. A sense of freedom to enjoy ourselves was our main priority.

Departure day finally arrived. After a leisurely farewell lunch with Barry, my husband, I entered the first stage of the long journey – a four hour bus ride from Exeter to Heathrow Airport.

June had arranged to fly from Jersey to Gatwick, where she too, would board a bus to Heathrow and meet up with Alice, Sally, Sylvia and Carol, at approximately 5.30 p.m. They, in turn, had travelled on a pre-arranged shuttle flight to Heathrow from Manchester – a thirty minute drive from where they all lived – and due to circumstances beyond their control, would be killing time at the airport from late morning.

It was just approaching 7.00 p.m. when my bus reached its destination. The journey so far had been very relaxing, helped by the combination of an almost empty bus, light motorway traffic and still feeling replete from the satisfying lunch. A quick call on my ancient, brick-like mobile phone to June located an easy-to-find meeting place, at the terminal of departure.

Thinking that my siblings would be feeling equally relaxed, and even bored from sitting around for such a long time, I was surprised to find a hive of frantic activity. Alice and Sally were bent over their open suitcases grabbing armfuls of their carefully packed personal belongings and shoving them haphazardly into plastic bags. Apparently, after being allowed to check-in early, the same considerate assistant advised that their overlarge suitcases were grossly overweight. Not wanting to forgo a percentage of their spending money before they'd even set foot on Australian soil, they were desperately trying to redistribute that weight.

In the event, my luggage was underweight, so I became the main recipient of their excess. Also, as an added precaution against payment, several more carrier bags were produced by Alice (who always keeps a dozen or so in her large handbag, for emergencies) to be filled and distributed amongst us as hand luggage. The sense of freedom normally associated with the aftermath of 'checking-in' was lost. And, as we slowly moved towards 'airport security', the x-ray conveyor belt looked more like the checkout tills of Tesco – especially as most of the carrier bags bore their name.

With a collective sigh of relief we emerged into the departure lounge unmolested, but soon realised that Sally was missing. She'd been singled out for bag searching and body frisking. A plastic comb with a thin metal handle was the item under suspicion. The authorities obviously thought that this sixty-two-year old woman, armed with her nine inch plastic and steel comb, was a potential threat. Whilst I would have dumped the offending item in the nearest dustbin, Sally was determined to hang onto it, sealing her own fate of stop and search at every check point between Heathrow and Sydney.

I had offered (and it was gladly accepted) to take on the role of organising the choice of airline and booking the flight. My intention, obviously, was getting the best deal for us and making absolutely sure that we were allocated seats together along the same row, positioning myself at the end of the row, next to my oldest and quietest sister.

A flurry of excitement accompanied the boarding and the finding of our allotted seats. But my excitement began to waver as droves of families with young children (and babies, would you believe) squeezed along the aisles, filling the entire plane. Concern completely banished the excitement, when I thought of the countless scenarios of disturbance that could erupt from every quarter of our confined, shared space, due to the demands of the very young.

In spite of my misgivings I reasoned that because the time was now way past 10 p.m. – and all small children should already be in dreamland – it would be prudent to proceed with my own preparations for sleep. On a long haul flight getting a reasonable amount of sleep is essential, and because I was still relatively relaxed and detached from the chaos around me, I felt confident about getting my quota.

After slipping on my inflated neck pillow – supplied with relaxing lavender oil inserted into its front panel – I positioned the bright green complimentary eye pads on my forehead, ready to drop down over my eyes, at the appropriate time. Next came the matching bright green complimentary bed socks – rolled on over the skin tight flight stockings – to help produce a cosy, 'I'm-in-bed' feeling. Finally, after wrapping the vivid orange flight blanket tightly around me, I very carefully released one hand and pressed the reclining button of my seat. Nothing happened. I pressed, prodded, wriggled and fiddled, until finally, I had to accept that I would be sleeping bolt upright. Hidden behind the multi-coloured coverings I silently seethed at my misfortune. All around me I heard seats being released into comfortable sleep-mode positions. At one point, I received a sharp smack on the forehead from the reclined seat in front – my own fault for not lifting the eye pads as I leaned forward a couple of inches.

Ten hours later – and still in the same bolt upright position – I'd disappointingly only passed through several twilight stages of sleep. The majority of that time, although

9

my eyes were blanked out, I was aware of what was happening around me. My sisters marvelled at how I could sleep so soundly in this position and one voice offered the opinion that maybe I was in a meditating trance. 'Yes girls, I heard the whispers, but believe me, I wasn't getting the restful slumber you were all so envious of.' I know too, that you weren't getting any sleep at all, thanks to the press-button seduction of the onboard entertainment; or in the case of Sylvia, the pack of cards that she kept about her, even when travelling. Still, at least I was resting. They, on the other hand, were in a permanent state of hypertension and over the next few days they would suffer the consequences. I had tried to pass on the wisdom of my previous experience of a long haul flight, but to no avail. That, along with the advice of not drinking too much alcohol, just fell on deaf ears.

The forty-five minute stop at Hong Kong airport passed in a haze of semi-consciousness. Two of our number were desperate to use the loo, but an even greater desperation was the need to stick together at all cost, so the majority of the forty-five minutes was used up locating and making use of the ladies-room facilities. We were tired and rumpled and the idea of a leisurely wash and brush up – to help rekindle a holiday mood – seemed like a good idea.

On returning to our seats, we noticed that the plane was now only about a third full. Two thirds of its precious space was up for grabs to the more streetwise traveller with sleep on their mind. This new scenario helped to lift my spirits, as I planned my strategy for when we were airborne and the seat belt lights went out. Armed with at least four vivid orange blankets, my eye pads, socks and a pile of flight pillows, I lay horizontal for the first time in twenty-four hours.

This golden opportunity, this gift from the Gods, was short lived. A combination of turbulence and the consequent irritating bleep of the seat belt sign lighting up, then the cabin staff insisting that the belt be worn in a sitting position (God knows why that should be safer than lying down, wrapped in several layers of soft blanket), shattered my earlier hopes. Plus, I had unwittingly made my cosy bed right at the back of the plane – for maximum privacy – realizing too late that it was only inches away from a toilet. I had a constantly changing audience witnessing my undignified attempt, at alternately lying then sitting, whilst blindfolded and tightly bound in orange blankets. One little boy, with the innocence and loud voice of the very young; pointed at me saying, 'That lady looks like a mummy from a tomb.' His mother shushed him, but not before all the heads in a ten yard radius turned to latch on to this little light entertainment. I almost spat at the boy, before remembering that I was a fifty-seven-year old grandmother; instead I pulled down my eye pads and ignored the lot of them.

After dozing for too short a time, I was woken by the clatter of breakfast being served. Reluctantly, I left my lying position and joined my sisters back at our allotted seats.

Even though most of the passengers were tired and pasty-faced, a mounting sense of excitement filled the air, as we made our descent into a country as far away from home as you can get.

3

Thankful for the abundance of trolleys for our retrieved luggage, and trying not to look how we felt, we emerged into the bright, sunny arrival lounge of Sydney Airport. Lilian, wearing an equally bright, sunny smile stood waiting with George. With her camera to the ready and an armful of 'Hawaiian' style garlands playfully thrown around our heads, we were led outside to be photographed several times. It was a relief to be here at last, it was also lovely to see Lilian and George looking bronzed and healthy, fresh and well rested. In contrast, we must have looked diabolical; we certainly felt it. Nevertheless, we all donned our broadest, albeit artificial, smiles and allowed the camera to record this very special occasion.

Half an hour later and we were still standing on the same spot of airport car park, watching George turning more crimson by the minute. We all knew in our hearts that there was no way he was going to get our entire luggage into two cars, but nobody had the energy or the guts to contradict his efforts. I'm usually up front for helping in any situation but as I watched George risk a self-inflicted hernia, by putting in, then taking out(at least four times) suitcases large enough to house a family of Pygmies; I just stood and watched in a semi-comatose stupor.

June thankfully took the initiative, even though she had had no sleep at all during the long journey. And a collective sigh of relief was heard, when she said quite boldly, 'I'm going to find a taxi to use for the largest suitcases, and we'll let the taxi driver do the lifting.' George's frustration and relief were intertwined with another emotion, dented pride, and reading the unspoken words that passed between him and his wife, I was encouraged to follow June, to search for a taxi.

Arriving at, and remaining in, the 'deluxe cabins' of the tourist park was to be the extent of today's activities (or so we thought). It was mid morning, ample time to catch a few hours sleep before unpacking and sorting out our belongings. Come the evening, we could then enjoy a couple of drinks to prepare us for a normal nights rest. But Lilian – exuberant and energetic – had alternative plans for the day. Without a hint of resistance from anyone, she whisked us all off to her house, allowing just enough time to drop our luggage inside the cabin and peel off the flight socks; which were stubbornly trying to remain bonded to our swollen feet and ankles.

Two hours later, and Lilian had become even more exuberant. Her cheery voice read out the neatly typed itinerary that she had carefully put together, listing all the places that we were intended to visit. This itinerary – a copy of which was handed to each one of us – included every day of our three week trip, with a time scale for each proposed visit. I glanced around at the five, lack lustre faces and knew, like me, they couldn't comprehend a single word of it; especially after drinking the two glasses of champagne that had complimented our hostess's pre organised buffet lunch.

After returning Lilian's lovely home to the spick and span condition we'd found it in – prior to eating and drinking the entire content of her laid out dining table – we were ushered again into their two cars. With George in the lead, we were driven for several hours, to several places – none of which has stayed in our memory – because we were all sleep walking.

Even the expectation of a quiet evening in turned out to be a pipe dream. We were taken to the local RSL club for drinks and an evening meal, before being escorted back to our accommodation. This was Lilian, introducing us to our new

13

lives for the next three weeks. She returned to her comfortable bed in leafy Lugarno, while we stood in our new abode; not yet unpacked, not enough room to put everything, if we did unpack, wondering what the hell we were doing here.

The next day is a series of lucid periods, interspersed with foggy daydreams. I remember waking at 5 a.m., deftly rolling out of the bottom bunk and finding Alice already awake and putting on the kettle. It was dark outside, so the sunshine and blue skies, which were a forgone conclusion of this trip, were still unverifiable. Nevertheless, the sound of a kettle being filled and the rattle of cups, brought on a homely, positive feeling, encouraging me to inject some extra gusto into my 'Good morning, Alice'.

Lilian, again our Good Samaritan, had stocked the fridges in both cabins with essentials, such as milk, bread, eggs, etc. but today we would need to shop for more groceries. She had mentioned that there was a supermarket barely five minutes walk from here, so as Alice and I drank our early morning cuppa, we planned our first shopping trip.

During the previous evening, we had all agreed to keep a kitty purse, into which we each put 50 dollars. This fund would be used for such things as provisions, bus fares, laundry, etc. and would be replenished by us all, as and when necessary. For some unknown reason I was given charge of this kitty purse, so after drinking our tea and quietly getting dressed, Alice and I set out with it in the direction of the supermarket, leaving Sally and our three sisters next door, still fast asleep.

The rest of the morning passed in a haze of eating breakfast, showering and unpacking (not necessarily in that order). But clear in my mind, are the rising stress levels when we realized the impossibility of finding enough space to house all our clothes; never mind the shoes, bags, beachwear and the endless bottles of shampoos, conditioners, sun oils and other bottles of God knows what! We didn't need all this surplus stuff, but frustratingly, we still needed to find room for it.

Suddenly, the stress levels really cranked up, when we heard a knock on the door accompanied by Lil's ready-for-action voice calling, 'Good morning campers, time for walkies.' As if playing a well choreographed game of statues we froze, and in that moment of silence and stillness I clearly heard the 'F' word being aggressively used in the cabin next door. I knew Sylvia was the culprit; her voice carries for miles, even in a gale force wind. Another phrase followed even more clearly than the first. 'We're not bloody kids,' confirming that it definitely was Sylvia; I'd heard her say this several times earlier.

Most of my sisters wouldn't use the 'F' word. Personally, I've never spoken the whole word out loud. It's a throwback to our years growing up, when we wouldn't even risk saying, 'bloody' or 'bugger' in front of Mum, even when we were old enough to bring in a wage. As a child, if ever there was a row at home, and the forbidden word was frustratingly shouted from Dad's lips, I immediately made myself scarce. Depending on the time of day, I would either scurry off to bed, go for a long walk or hide in the coal shed, where I would nervously munch my way through a lump of nutty slack. Using that forbidden word would fire up Mum's temper and everyone in the vicinity would suffer for it. Both parents have been dead for some time now, but I still refuse to use that word.

Lilian remained cheerful and ready for action. Maybe she hadn't heard the hurtful comment; which meant she'd gone deaf overnight, or maybe the embarrassing phrases I'd just heard were commonplace here in Australia. We, in our cabin, being the oldest, the quietest, and possessing the most self-control, said nothing. But our thoughts were just as treacherous – using the 'F' word is not the only way to release frustration. We offered Lilian a cup of tea to stall her a little. She declined, saying she'd had her breakfast and her café latte; which meant she was really revved up and ready to go.

4

The sun shone brightly between clusters of ominous looking clouds, reminding me of how it would probably be back in England. Lowering my eyes to the surrounding gardens – full of unfamiliar, tropical plants – brought me back to the reality of where I was.

We were on our way to the local beach. Lilian, marching ahead, was also giving us a tour of the neighbourhood. Like the perfect guide, her arms were gesticulating in all directions, as she pointed out everything – and I mean everything – along the way. We, in contrast to her bubbly, skip along manner, quietly followed her lead, lost in our own thoughts. Mine were to get to the beach, lay down my towel and shut out the world for a couple of hours.

A ripple of excitement passed between us as we finally stepped onto the beach, with the vastness of the beautiful, blue ocean stretched out before us. It was a joy to kick off my sandals and feel the warm, gritty sand caress each toe. But as I reached into my bag for the towel which would provide the means to expand on that joy, Lilian's forthright voice announced, 'We're not finished yet.'

That same forthright voice informed us that a short walk along the beach to our neighbouring suburb of Brighton-le-Sands was next on the agenda. The main reason for this walk, she informed, was to help get our circulation back on an even footing and prevent any side effects from the long haul flight. In short, the walk was for our benefit, not hers.

We acquiesced, but I remained barefoot as we walked along the beach; a silent protest that both slowed me down and allowed the natural warmth of the sand to relax and assuage my disappointment. The others remained shod – maybe this too was a silent protest – the intrusion of sand entering sandals must have been uncomfortable, a self-

17

imposed punishment, for not having the guts or energy to stand up to their own kin, whose dominance seemed all powerful.

Lilian's short walk, turned out to be a bloody (sorry Mum) long trek! Exhaustion – due mainly to the soft blanket of jetlag descending and wrapping around us once again – was apparent on all but one face. We also felt very hungry, so it was a great relief to stop at a beachside café and have lunch. Fortunately we were served promptly, except for Sally, who for some reason seemed to have been forgotten. Still smarting from the constant attention at the airports, Sally was in no mood to be singled out again. She hot footed it up to the counter and demanded to know where her meal was, just as the waiter arrived at the table with it. Lilian's light-hearted remark to the waiter, 'Typical whinging Pom,' didn't produce the intended result.

Suddenly, the unthinkable happened. It started to pour down. Sheets of rain fell from the heavens, turning the overhead sun shades, into very welcome umbrellas. We sat for a while, not caring whether the rain stopped or not. It seemed more important to scupper Lilian's plans, than to waste an afternoon in weather that we'd flown across the world to escape. The rain didn't stop, and eventually we found ourselves on a bus, dripping wet and heading back to our disorganised shacks.

Our shack – which was crowded enough with three – had seven of us crammed into it and the astronomical rise in humidity from our damp clothes, created an air of claustrophobia and restlessness. The day was still young as far as Lilian was concerned, and she soon got into her stride outlining all the options available on a wet afternoon, unperturbed by the atmospherics of her surroundings.

'I've got too much to do next door.' This simple, softly spoken statement came from Carol, my youngest sister, and without waiting for any response, she opened the door to leave. June and Sylvia, suddenly alerted to this opportunity of escape, leapt up and sidled out behind her, mumbling their apologies but clearly relieved to be off.

Lilian suggested an afternoon at the cinema. Sally, still smarting from the earlier comment of 'Whinging Poms' and encouraged by the insubordination of Carol, said pointedly, as she waved her arms around her, 'I can't sit and relax in a bloody cinema, when I've still got all this unpacking to do.' Alice nodded in agreement, but said nothing. I, on the other hand, had finished my unpacking, having brought only a small suitcase and very few cosmetics. The thought of an afternoon in a dark cinema seemed like the perfect environment to snatch a little nap, so with an air of magnanimity I agreed to join Lilian, leaving Sally and Alice the time and peace they needed to get straight.

A deep sense of hurt and disappointment coursed through me as I was given a guided tour around the much tidier and neatly organised shack. Alice happily pointed out 'her spaces', which managed to house everything that she'd crammed into her coffin-sized suitcase and half a dozen carrier bags. Sally, in perfect parrot fashion, repeated and pointed out 'her spaces', but concluded – with a hang-dog expression – that she was forced to keep some of her tops in a suitcase under the bed, otherwise there would have been no space at all for my stuff.

My stuff – which I'd left neatly organised and taking up one third of the shack's available storage space – had been shifted and squeezed into the smallest of hanging and cupboard areas. The hurt and disappointment erupted into complaints; but my angry outburst was crushed under their unbelievable point of view that they had more stuff, so needed more space.

I kicked off my wet shoes not caring where they landed and flung my shower proof jacket over a chair, then watched as it slipped to the floor in a slow, fluid motion which left a trail of rain droplets down the chair leg. A flush of pleasure hit me, as their faces registered that I wasn't about to remedy this physical slur on their newly organised environment. Stepping over the wet heap I retreated to the anti-room, sliding the door forcefully behind me.

Lying down on the middle bunk, I was all set for a long haul of self-pity, but before I had taken the first step on the downward spiral Sally slid open the door I'd just slammed shut. 'We're out on the town tonight, you haven't got time to lie there you need to start getting ready.'

'I'm knackered,' I blurted out without turning to face her.

'How can you be knackered when you've been sitting on your arse all afternoon enjoying yourself?' I didn't respond – afraid I might say something which I later would have to apologise for – instead I returned to the downward spiral.

I *was* sitting on my arse, while the carve up of territory was going on in the shack, but I certainly wasn't enjoying myself. The whole afternoon had been one big disappointment, and until ten minutes ago when Lilian dropped me off on her way back home, I'd been looking forward to getting back here.

The film Lilian and I had decided to watch was 'The Pacifier.' Just the thing, I'd thought, to help me slip into the arms of Morpheus. Unfortunately, the cinema was filled with school children, who'd created such a din as they munched

20

and slurped their way through a mountain of edible goodies. Undeterred, I'd waited patiently for the lights to dim and the film to start, which would hopefully call a halt to the constant chatter and flicking of popcorn.

For a blissful few seconds we were plunged into darkness and silence followed for a few seconds more. Then with the volume turned up to a deafening pitch – killing stone-dead any thought of snoozing – the film began.

The main actor – an American, whose name I have no wish to remember – was every bit as raucous as the family of children he was meant to pacify and organise. When the film finally ended, Lilian shouted over the clapping audience, 'That's not one George would enjoy.' I felt I had at least one ally in this alien world.

'There's a cup of tea and some ham butties for you Marg.' Sally's voice rang out, bringing me back to where I was – in prone position on the middle bunk. The shortened version of my name was a sure sign that forgiveness and endearment was on offer, as well as the tea and ham butties. We had a tendency to shorten our names; especially at times when friendship and affection prevailed, or, if we wanted to borrow something. Although none of us had long, complicated Christian names, nor did we possess middle names (except for Sylvia, who was expected to be the last born and was probably given a middle name in a flurry of relief that the long line of babies had come to an end).

Nevertheless, this had been the first time since our arrival that I had heard it, reminding me that not a single one of us had yet shortened Lilian's name to the customary Lil.

In a soft friendly tone Alice was now asking for my opinion on which of the many dozen necklaces she ought to wear, in relation to one of her many dozen tops. They were clearly trying their best to smooth over the earlier tension. I decided to take advantage of this by grabbing the shower first, but I was informed – again, in a soft friendly manner – that they'd showered whilst I was out at the pictures (sitting on my arse was diplomatically left out of the statement).

With tea and butties consumed and body freshly showered, I felt much more positive towards the evening ahead. After all, the cabin was full to bursting with fancy clothes and several kilos of bling-bling, why not put it to good use and get 'Dolled Up'. An exciting and energetic night out would be just the thing to keep us awake until normal bedtime, ensuring a good long sleep. Then bright and early tomorrow, we would be all set for the next column of the typed itinerary: APRIL 13TH – A DAY IN THE HEART OF SYDNEY (experiencing all its wonderful sights).

5

Glass doors led immediately into the heart of the large public house. The dim lighting, designed to create an atmosphere of intimacy in the spacious bar, couldn't hide the fact that the place was almost empty. An open archway leading off the spacious bar revealed a few faces – eyes riveted in concentration on the moving images of the slot machines before them. They were too preoccupied to register our arrival and we weren't interested enough in the gambling room to join them.

Huddled together and feeling very conspicuous in our frills and glitter, we were uncertain about which of the many vacant tables to head for. There were no more than nine – very casually dressed – people in this large, dimly lit space, but it felt like a thousand eyes were locked onto us. Lilian broke the impasse, 'I've never actually been in here before, but I think there's a quiz, tonight.' She confidently led us up a broad stairway that led to an upper floor, causing me to wonder if she had in fact been here before – not necessarily to spend the evening – but as preliminary research for her itinerary. The space above was a perfect replica of the bar below, right down to the lack of customers.

Within minutes of sitting at our chosen table – waiting for a much needed drink – we were approached by an overexcited young woman, bearing a Cheshire cat grin and an armful of paraphernalia. She was the organiser of the quiz and this was her big chance to almost double the head count of contestants for her imminent competition. Before we knew fully what was happening, paperwork and pens were placed before us.

All eyes fell on Lilian, whose bright, positive, smiling face was looking at the first sheet of questions, titled: Australian General Knowledge. It was obvious that she knew the answers. Looking at the same questions only produced confusion in the rest of us. I rummaged for my glasses, but found they only helped to make more glaringly obvious, how little I knew of the place we'd be living for the next three weeks.

The next round of the quiz – announced by the overexcited young woman – would be verbal questions on worldwide general knowledge, followed by questions on popular music. She looked directly at our table with an encouraging smile. I really did admire her determination to keep us on board, especially after our pathetic results of the first round.

Two large bowls of hot snacks and a second round of drinks were produced by Lilian, either as an incentive to rescue the diminishing camaraderie or to provide sustenance to activate the brain cells before the next onslaught. Whatever the intention, the refreshments were accepted with relish and consumed before the next round began.

Not wanting to appear completely gormless in the eyes of these few Australians, we followed Lilian's example of sitting straight backed, with our pens eagerly poised over the sheet of blank paper. But tensions began to rise again as Lilian's quick response to most of the questions began to irritate and alienate us from the game. Even the popular music questions seemed to be of an era that was unfamiliar to all but one of us.

Sensing the developing situation the quiz organizer surreptitiously started to give hints to the answers and when this wouldn't or couldn't bring forth a result, she blatantly wrote some of the answers down for us. There was a brief moment of satisfaction when a disagreement between Lilian and June, on one of the answers, proved June to be right.

But, at the final count, the Ozzies had wiped the floor with us, in spite of the efforts of our brainiest sister.

This was definitely not the sort of evening we'd had in mind and as disappointment, frustration and tiredness began to take its toll, venomous vibrations filled the air. Wisely, Lilian decided it was time for her to return to the welcoming arms of George. She had brought three of us here in her car with a taxi carrying the other three, but that helpful gesture was not on offer now.

It's firmly acknowledged that Lilian is the most educated of our family. The countless, successfully completed college courses – obtained mainly whilst living in Australia – plus a degree in Business Management, helped her climb the ladder of her chosen career. All credit to her, the years of hard work had paid off. But she'd be the first to admit that choosing not to have children, had made this much easier to achieve. As for the rest of us; we started our families whilst we were still young and naïve, content to leave all thoughts of schooling behind us.

I changed my view and gained a place at Art College back in 1979 when my son and daughter were nine and eleven years old, respectively. Being a mature student helped me to see the wisdom of being given a second chance at further education – and to embark on a creative journey that's been both satisfying and life-style enhancing.

'All sisters argue sometimes, it doesn't mean anything,' Alice had said, in a soothing voice, trying her best to stem the tears that had rolled down Carol's anguished face. Carol might be the youngest of the bunch, and doesn't look anywhere near her age of forty- two, but having raised five children – the eldest in his early twenties – to my mind, gave her every right to understand and be disappointed in the current situation.

'I've really been looking forward to this trip. I love you all so much and all I wanted was for us to share three weeks of happiness. Lilian thinks I'm stupid for not getting educated enough to have a good job, instead of having children.' She'd sobbed. Then added, 'And I miss my kids so much.'

'Where is that soddin' taxi?' had been Sylvia's impatient response, 'Let's get her home and into bed, she'll be fine tomorrow.'

'I wish I was really going home, to my own bed,' Sally had added, wistfully.

'Don't you start lady,' cut in Alice, before silence descended in the almost deserted bar, where we'd sat waiting to be taken back to the shacks.

I was fifteen years old when Carol was born. Alice and Sally were both married with homes of their own, leaving me the position of eldest girl. Suddenly I'd become general helper and chief babysitter – a role that was bitterly resented.

By the time Carol was three years old I, too, had flown the nest; filled with hopes of travelling the world. Visiting some of the exotic sounding places that I'd come across on the atlas pages of my geography book at school cancelled out any thoughts of possible homesickness. What transpired were a couple of years working in Pontin's holiday camps – the most exotic being located in Jersey.

Although Jersey wasn't the other side of the world, the sense of freedom I'd experienced, and the crowd of like-minded friends that I made, more than made up for the lack in distance. During this time of complete self-reliance I gained confidence, financial reward and most of all, total

privacy. It was wonderful to be able to tidy away my
personal belongings and clothes, knowing that they'd still be
there when I needed them. Back home, in those far-off days,
begging, borrowing and even stealing, was rife.

The downside to this new-found freedom was the missing
out on bonding with the younger members of my family as
they were growing up.

I never again went back to Lancashire to live, choosing
instead to settle much further south with my husband Barry
and our two children; visiting my northern family on special
occasions but never staying for longer than a week.

As I looked at Carol's lovely, tearful face, I remembered
the babe-in-arms from over forty years ago, feeling the loss
of the many unshared years. 'I'm so sorry,' I'd whispered,
reaching out to hold her close – at that moment loving her
more than anything in the world – and mentally thanking
Mum and Dad for giving her life. After releasing her, I
vowed silently to make the most of this precious time
together.

'Don't worry about it Marg, she always gets emotional
after a few drinks, she'll be as right as rain tomorrow. Where
is, that soddin' taxi?' And, as if in response to Sylvia's very
audible words, a loud beep signalled the arrival of our
transport home.

The illuminated clock on the cooker read 5.25 a.m. Had I
really only spent fifty minutes reliving the last few days? A
fundamental difference in the atmosphere of the shack
caused my body to stiffen involuntarily. The room was now
deathly quiet! No soft snoring or snuffles came from the
bunk bed area and an absolute silence had taken over the half
of the double bed where Alice lay…!! A picture of her

27

battered face appeared before my tightly closed eyes. I Reached across blindly to touch her; at the same time praying aloud to Jesus, Mary and God almighty himself, for her not to be dead. My prayers were answered with a loud snort, as warm flesh was squeezed. Euphoric with relief, but disappointed that neither of my sisters were awake to share it, forced me to settle back into my own thoughts.

The room was silent again; surely now was the best chance to get some sleep. But deep down I knew that I would have to relive the day of the thirteenth too, before I could find any real peace of mind that would lead to slumber.

6

As I recall, we had all managed to get some quality sleep on Tuesday, the night of the twelfth, so being ready for an early start the next morning wasn't too difficult.

Our orders were to travel to the nearby town of Hurstville, by bus. The appropriate bus stop had been pointed out to us by Lilian the day before, accompanied by the words, 'Don't forget, this is the bus stop for Hurstville.' We hadn't forgotten, and we had all arrived at the designated place at the pre-arranged time. Once in the safety of Lilian's charge, we handed over the reigns of responsibility to her for the rest of the journey to Sydney.

Circular Quay was our destination and the use of the rail network was to be our means of getting there. The weather forecast had been good and I was looking forward to relaxing and enjoying the sights, in the company of my six sisters. Remembering the vow of the previous evening, I was determined to let nothing spoil this day.

After disembarking into the relative gloom of Circular Quay Station, we were led through a series of walkways and moving staircases. Our pace was brisk and in the main we'd walked in single file. Every so often Lilian had found it necessary to stop and allow the last two in our line to catch up, until suddenly we'd emerged into sunshine so brilliant we were all stopped dead in our tracks.

The glittering water of Sydney Harbour was spread before us and the bright sunrays bearing down from the cloudless sky reflected off every wave and ripple across its surface. Lilian had obviously enjoyed this spectacle many times and was well aware of its impact, so a minute or two was allowed for us to capture the scene on our cameras.

A nearby street entertainer – sprayed from head to toe in gold paint and posing as a living statue – was the next attraction that caught our eye as he shimmered in the sunshine. In turn, each of us had moved in close to the poised, still form to have our photograph taken and each of us had rewarded him, by placing a dollar in the already positioned, outstretched palm. A gleeful wink had been our reward and the only sign of movement by the entertainer – six winks for six dollars, (Lilian abstained, anxious to move on).

To prevent any further delay we were then led at breakneck speed to see Sydney Opera House, glancing quickly sideways on the way, as Lilian's arms, aided by her voice, pointed out the Harbour Bridge. Deprived of enough time to appreciate this glorious scene my attention remained locked on the crowds of tourists that slowed our progress. Envy and irritation had coursed through me, as they intermittently paused for a while to appreciate the lovely, peaceful waters that reflected this famous landmark.

Marching at the pace of soldiers on parade, we were then led up the steps of the Sydney Opera House – to allow for photographs of us in its foreground. Three minutes later we were down the steps, photographing each other with this monumental piece of architecture viewed in the background. Then it had been full steam ahead back in the direction of the station, with all eyes riveted on Lilian's back – which seemed to be getting way ahead of us.

I'd developed a stitch and I'd heard several of the girls saying they'd needed the loo. This might have been a ploy for a crafty sit down. It didn't work, Lilian was relentless in her marching and we needed to keep her in our sights. She had mentioned earlier an open-topped-tour bus, which would travel around the parts of Sydney that even she couldn't march through, and it was the boarding point for this bus that she was now desperately trying to locate.

A mixture of appetising aromas filled the air as our marching bodies cut a swathe through the milling tourists, deciding on which of the many restaurants could best satisfy their needs. One or two members of our group had begun to mumble about their hunger. I was ravenous, and I hadn't lowered my voice as I'd announced it, hoping it would reach the head of our line. Lilian had looked back and slowed her pace, allowing us to catch up with her. 'One of the early stop offs of the tour bus is a visit to a very famous Pie & Mash kiosk,' she'd said encouragingly, when we were all in ear shot. Some of the gang had been content with this and a new lease of life was injected into their marching. I'd been disappointed but remained silent, choosing to look longingly at the bistros, tappas bars and the wide range of fish restaurants serving up between them, every delectable dish you could think of.

We had discovered with great pleasure that eating out in Australia was inexpensive and good value for money, with portions usually large enough for two. I hadn't travelled across the world, to indulge in pie and mash – I'd been more than happy to leave that sort of food behind for the colder months in England.

With an air of anarchy about them Alice and Sylvia had started to dawdle, saying that they weren't especially hungry. Sally cut in with, 'You've both got enough spare weight to last a week without eating.' This hadn't helped to alleviate their obvious tiredness, nor had it added anything to the dwindling family companionship. 'Hostile' was the best word to describe our feelings, as we'd climbed the stairs of the open-topped, red, tour bus. Unlike eating out, the charge for the bus tour wasn't cheap. But as none of us knew yet what to expect, there wasn't a single word of protest as the kitty purse was half empted – although a few knowing looks left no one in any doubt that this bus tour was bloody expensive. The upper floor had been empty, giving us the opportunity to disperse like strangers, seeking their own private territory. Silence pervaded for several minutes, as we'd pretended to be interested in the surrounding stationary buildings. Then, with a collective sigh of relief, the bus moved slowly forward.

A well-honed voice – carried through a plastic, speaker-box – pointed out the places of interest in downtown Sydney, giving us a legitimate reason to remain silent, although no one was concentrating on what was said. In spite of this obvious lack of interest, Lilian continued to play the perfect guide. Her arms shot out in the direction of each spoken highlight on the tour, to make sure that we didn't miss any of it. After several cursory glances at some of Sydney's prestigious buildings, we reached the famous Pie & Mash kiosk.

Freed from the tension of feigning interest, I'd volunteered to secure a long bench looking out over the inlet of ocean that bordered this part of Sydney, whilst my sisters queued for their choice of food at the kiosk. As well as hoping that the usual calming effect of water would work its magic on us, by scrutinizing their plates as they returned, I'd be given the chance to select the most appealing looking pie from the limited selection on offer – although by this time, I could have eaten a horse!

Each harbouring thoughts that were surely alien to a family outing, on a lovely sunny day, we sat quietly eating. The void of silence was filled by the high-pitched calls of seagulls circling above, and as they'd landed to mop up the crumbs and leftovers of the feeding public, this too had allowed us a diversion to concentrate on, which seemed preferable to conversation. The food was delicious, just as

Lilian had promised, although none of us had had the grace to admit it. Every scrap of it had been eaten, leaving the entertaining seagulls without their due.

Having spent the last few hours without the chance to use a toilet, the need to do so now was pretty urgent. Lilian had been sitting next to me and the long silence was broken when I'd asked her where the nearest toilet was. She'd stood up to look around her and as she'd turned with her back towards me I'd noticed several dollops of sickly green seagull pooh on the lower backside of her crisp, white shorts. My fist automatically went to my mouth, to stifle a laugh. Then I felt torn between bringing everyone else into this humorous development, or telling Lilian discreetly to save further embarrassment. Whatever the decision, I'd have to act quickly before she plonked herself down again and made the mess even worse.

My dilemma was short lived. Sally had also noticed the offending patches of digested mushy peas. Her decision to tell had been instantaneous and indiscreet, and her loud sniggers set me off laughing uncontrollably. Fortunately, Lilian had been too preoccupied to notice, as she hot footed it to the nearest hotel toilet, hands held behind her, desperately trying to hide the patches without actually touching them.

I'd been just about to follow Lilian – at a more sedate pace – when Sylvia and Carol approached me. They'd decided to go into the heart of Sydney, to locate a mobile phone shop. Sylvia's daughter-in-law was about to give birth and she'd been finding it difficult to phone home on her mobile. I'd heard snippets of conversations earlier, about the frustrations of not being able to phone home, but I honestly hadn't been interested enough to take much notice. It seemed important now to pay more attention.

Usually, Sylvia is a larger-than-life character and a born comedian. Whenever you're in her company, wall-to-wall laughter is guaranteed. I have held my aching sides on many an occasion, begging for her to stop her verbal antics. But standing before me in the light of the midday sun she'd looked a shadow of her former, funny self. I'd asked her why it was necessary to use a mobile phone, when surely a landline would be more dependable and less costly. Her response had been a blank stare.

They all know my views on mobile phones; I own one, but use it for emergencies only. It was used to locate my sisters at Heathrow and it will get used again when I get back to England – to let Barry know in good time of my arrival – so that he can be there to meet me. Naturally I rang him from Lilian's home when we first arrived, to reassure him that we'd arrived safely. For me that's enough phoning, thank you very much. Enjoying where I am, and not even thinking about where I'm from, is to my mind, what a holiday is all about.

For the rest of my sisters who have made this trip, mobile phones have become a part of their every day life and dress. The colourful, covered slabs of metal, suspended from matching coloured cords, are slipped over their heads whenever we venture out of doors, even when going down to the beach. Exchanging text messages seems to have become an obsession that's taken over a large chunk of their waking hours; satisfying an insatiable need to know every little detail about the weather, the latest football scores, or any other trivia that's happening on the other side of the globe.

When Lilian returned – cardigan tied casually around her waist to cleverly hide the inevitable wet patch – she was confronted with Sylvia and her determined venture. To be fair, Lilian had offered to accompany Sylvia and Carol, saying that she would probably locate a phone shop much quicker than they would, but Sylvia had flatly refused. 'We'll just jump on the next tour bus, get off at the High Street, go straight to a phone shop and jump on the next bus back. Where's the problem with that?' Evidently, no one at the time could see a problem with that, because there was no response (not even from Lilian). After watching the pair mount the next bus, we'd walked around the corner to an open- fronted bar and settled down with a cold drink to await their return.

Two hours had passed and we were still waiting. The relaxing effect of the couple of cool drinks had long since worn off, along with the attempt at tentative conversation. Even the chance of catching up with the rest of the tour – which had included a stop off at the beautiful Darling Harbour – was slipping away with the sunny afternoon that had so far been spent pacing up and down the same twenty yard stretch of concrete. Plus, we were all mindful of the goodly sum we'd paid to see those sights.

In frustration, Sally had started finger punching on her beloved mobile phone. I think the words, 'Where the hell are you?' in shortened form, were blasted towards Sylvia's phone. Within a few minutes a wonderful beep beep sound, indicated a reply.

'We are on bus now,' Sally had read out with relief and the slight hint of a smile.

'Well thank goodness for mobile phones,' I'd responded, in an effort to lighten the situation. All eyes focussed on the busy road and in particular, every moving vehicle that was red.

Another fifty minutes of frustration passed before we received a further text message from Sylvia. They were now off the bus – turned off by the driver – because their tickets were no longer valid. Within ten seconds of receiving this confusing text I'd scrutinised my own ticket, which was stamped quite clearly – VALID 24HRS. We began to wonder if the two of them had decided on an afternoon shopping spree, instead of returning to the strained atmosphere of our company, but we'd found it hard to believe that they would leave us hanging around here all this time, while they enjoyed themselves.

Forced into communicating, we'd decided that as the afternoon was almost over we would board the next available bus and meet them at Circular Quay and catch a train back home. Sally was holding all the return train tickets, so it was necessary to meet them. But as the shortened version of this decision was punched into the little phone through tightly clenched teeth, I'd wondered if one person holding all the tickets had been such a wise move.

Forty-five more minutes had been spent standing at the same bus stop before the next bus slowly came into view, twenty-five minutes later than it should have been. As it pulled in thirty yards beyond the bus stop, we'd run to it like a bunch of demented warriors, primed for war.

The same female bus driver who had dropped us there hours before stared defensively into five very angry faces, as each of us had presented our ticket pushed up to her nose, with a finger emphasising its validity. Four of us had then climbed the stairs, leaving Lilian to sort her out.

Again tension had reigned amongst us, but this time our vengeance was aimed at Sylvia. She had definitely been to blame for spoiling our afternoon.

But when Lilian had joined us upstairs and explained what had happened, we'd had to reconsider who was to blame. Apparently, this very same driver had put the two girls off the bus, saying their ticket was no longer valid. She'd then taken money off them later in the afternoon, to drop them off at Circular Quay. But the most crucial information – why had she done this? – hadn't been forth coming. I'd suggested taking her by the throat and shaking her until she coughed up the information. But Lil's response to my good idea had been a smile accompanying, 'Well at least I got a refund for the unnecessary charge to Circular Quay.'

The last part of the bus journey had passed mostly unnoticed, except for the aftermath of a road traffic accident, which had closed part of a busy main road. Maybe this had been the cause of all the problems; if so I'd felt no sympathy for those involved. I'd vowed only the day before to make the most of this trip. And there I'd sat, experiencing disappointment, anger and the tiredness of jetlag, which seemed to have descended suddenly. Someone was to blame for this bad day, maybe it was Lilian, maybe it was Sylvia, or the woman bus driver, but it certainly wasn't me.

It hadn't been difficult to pick out Sylvia and Carol amongst the hoards of people as we approached the entrance to Circular Quay Station. It also hadn't been difficult to see from their stance, that they were just as fed up as we were. We had done nothing wrong, but I knew with every fibre of my being, all hell was about to be let loose in our direction. Carol knew it too; the tears were already glistening in her eyes.

All the frustration and worry that Sylvia had bottled up over the last few days had been released in a tirade of obscenities, aimed in the direction of Lilian. Nothing had been held back – except her fists – thank God. Sally and June, who had been standing either side of Lilian, unconsciously took a step closer to her. We'd all known that Sylvia's reaction had been grossly unfair.

I'd approached Sylvia with the intention of asking her if she'd managed to get her phone sorted. But before I'd had a chance to speak, she'd turned to head for the train, leaving behind her an announcement that had caused dozens of heads to turn. 'We've spent all bloody day travelling from bus to train, then bus to more soddin' buses for what? pie and bloody mash.'

As we'd travelled back to Ramsgate locked once again in a strained silence, my thoughts were drawn towards the double bed, which would be mine for the first time that night. I'd thought about it a couple of times earlier in the day when things had got difficult, and as before, the thought had produced a little warm glow, which had helped to dispel the chill of the circumstances. I now had time to expand on those indulgent thoughts; which included a quiet evening reading my book, propped against a mountain of soft pillows, whilst lying in the vastness of crisp, white sheets. Maybe I'd have a glass of wine to soothe my jagged nerves, after such a difficult day. Then, heaven waited, in the form of a long comfortable nights rest.

Suddenly I'd felt caught in a mild hot flush; which usually meant, stress and brain overload. I'd turned to Lilian and asked her what night it was that George had booked the welcome meal. 'Tonight,' she'd said softly, before returning to her own thoughts. My thoughts, involving the relaxed evening reading, evaporated and were replaced with a possible nightmare scenario.

George had very generously booked a welcome meal for us at one of their favourite, local restaurants. He'd told us about it on our first day as we drove by the restaurant displaying a large blackboard that read *SIX SISTERS FROM ENGLAND WELCOME TO AUSTRALIA*, a very nice touch, I'd thought. And when booking this meal, he'd also shown sensitivity and consideration by allowing us three days to settle in. I'd turned to Lilian again and with genuine sympathy had said that maybe not all of us would be able to make it. Her response had been very simple, very dignified and very sad. 'George will naturally be disappointed, but he'll understand, if you can't all make it.'

We did all make it. Once we were back at the shacks several pep talks were exchanged between us, which led to a precarious truce. We'd all agreed that George didn't deserve to be let down. Within the hour, we had all showered and were ready to board the two taxis that were on their way, to transport us to George's favourite local restaurant.

It would be nice to romance a little and say that the meal was a great success, we'd all kissed and made up and enjoyed every minute of the evening. But a commitment to be truthful is a quirk of mine.

We'd had several photographs taken during that evening meal and of course we'll all be smiling for the camera. Yet I still cringe as I remember the surrounding whispers of how hard the spuds were, and the not so subtle shake of the heads when presented with slightly unfamiliar food; which in turn encouraged hushed, fearful remarks that they couldn't possibly eat it.

I'd thoroughly enjoyed my choice of meal; which fortunately, didn't contain any potatoes. But I did remember overhearing George's comments to Lilian that the standards weren't as good as usual. We'd all been together and communicating again, which had meant a lot to me, even though the term 'Whinging Poms' had floated uppermost in my thoughts several times. But as we rode back in the taxi, my thoughts had turned once again to the double bed waiting patiently for me to come home.

7

The sound of shuffling feet and a kettle being filled with water pulled me gently to the surface of consciousness. I lay still for a minute or two, allowing my thoughts to wrap around, where I was and what day I had woken into. All the events of the previous twenty-four hours passed before my closed eyes in compacted form. The couple of hours sleep I'd finally managed to embrace were enough to restore mind, body and spirit to an equilibrium I thought had deserted me forever.

Sally was the one doing the soft-shoe shuffle, whilst preparing to make a pot of tea. She was also doing a fair amount of muttering as she feverishly searched through a tray of medications that was worryingly too large for three people; and none of them belonged to me. Intrigued, I decided to remain still and watch her for a while. Her demeanour, which is normally upright and relaxed, had undergone a negative makeover. Taking into account the anger she must surely still harbour, at the untimely death of Penny, her face is usually smiling and serene and she is always the sister we turn to for a sympathetic ear. Could the last few days have altered her countenance so much?

'Good morning, Sally, did you get a good nights rest?' I asked, climbing out of bed as gently as possible, not wanting to disturb Alice. The look on her face gave me her answer in no uncertain terms. She carried on rifling through the plastic tray that contained pills of every shape and colour. At last she found what she was looking for and it was snatched up and held triumphantly in her closed fist, as if she'd found a long lost diamond from a favourite ring. Her hunched shoulders visibly relaxed and a partial smile crossed her face. 'I've had horrible indigestion all night, thanks to hard spuds and foreign food. I'll be fine now that I've found my pills.'

She held her closed fist aloft and wore an even broader smile – returning her face to the Sally that I knew and loved best.

We sat down at the small table, each fondling a hot mug of tea. Between sips I told her about Alice's mishap, and how surprised I was that she had managed to sleep through it, considering her intrusive indigestion. It soon became apparent that she knew all about what had happened to Alice, when she blatantly said, 'Oh, I heard her fall out of bed and start moaning. She only did it to get back in the double bed.'

'But she's got a badly cut mouth and extensive bruising to her body, no one in their right mind would do that on purpose; think of the pain.'

'Well I was in enough pain with this damned indigestion, so I kept my mouth shut and let you get on with it. Look at her, she's sleeping like a baby. I'm the one in pain – until these pills start to work.' I turned and looked at the sheet-covered mound that was Alice's foetal-positioned body; lying at the extreme edge of the large bed. The covers were pulled up to her ears, completely hiding all trace of the ugly bruising that will have developed over the last few hours.

Thursday the fourteenth was destined to be a beach day. The weather was perfect and after the rigours of yesterday, a five minute walk to soft golden sand was the only travelling we could stomach. The kitty purse was empty; in fact several of us were owed money, due to the expense of the previous day and the high cost of taxis in the evening. An economy drive was definitely on the cards today.

Having grown up in such a large family we'd all learnt about the value of money – or more precisely, the lack of it – at a very early age, and stretching every penny earned, borrowed or found became an art form. Whilst working in Jersey, at the holiday camp café, my ability to cut a tomato into twelve slices, along with several other cost-cutting skills – to fatten the profits of the management – earned me promotion to charge hand. This promotion naturally provided higher wages, half of which was sent home to help salve my guilty conscience for leaving the family with one less wage packet.

In comparison to those early years, we are all much more financially secure. But the ingrained ability to survive on next to nothing kicks in easily when the need arises.

It was unanimously decided that for the next couple of days at least, we would buy our food at the supermarket and cook at home using the facilities of the accommodation. Nothing would be spent on travelling costs, because we would explore and enjoy the local amenities. In short, we were to refrain from any unnecessary expenditure. This enforced self-control did not include alcohol – which, according to most of my sisters – is a necessity whilst on holiday. Debts were settled, the kitty purse was replenished and we felt that we could now move on and start to really enjoy our holiday.

As we'd boarded the taxis home on the previous evening, Lilian had tentatively suggested meeting at our local beach, but mindful of our mounting rebelliousness at being overly-organised, she hadn't stated a time. Although we'd settled down on our beach towels with a collective sigh of pleasure at the chance to relax at last, because after an hour Lilian hadn't yet arrived, we were all starting to feel a little sad, and more than a little concerned. She was the missing piece of a seven sided whole, and it didn't feel right that she wasn't here.

Analizing these feelings and being drawn into a discussion of our own behaviour since arriving in her homeland, only emphasized the concern – and the guilt.

After further consideration, we came to the conclusion that Lilian's only crime was in trying to show us too much, in too short a time. She is, after all, the family's main doer and organiser. Unfortunately, these virtues don't always sit well with the plodders or the strong-willed members of the family. The final consensus of opinion was: although her methods were sometimes downright exhausting, her intentions were always noble.

Who else in our enormous family, would, or could have, composed and read out the wonderful epitaph for Mum's funeral? Then four years later, it was taken for granted, that she would do the same for Dad. I watched her closely from the safety of the church pew, where I stood, arms linked with all my siblings. Although we were crying uncontrollably, Lil remained stoically self-possessed, even though we all knew, that like us, her heart was breaking.

'Lil's here,' rang through the air. The simplicity of the two words failed to hide the accompanying expression of relief and welcome. There was a reticence about her for about half an hour, but the constant use of her shortened name and some good natured fun and banter – at the expense of Alice and her nocturnal accident – soon melted this away.

The ocean temperature was perfect for swimming and even Alice, who can't swim, enjoyed frolicking about in the clear water, protected by a huge, black, rubber ring that looked more like a tyre from a tractor. This helped, no doubt, to take her mind off the cuts and bruises that had thankfully turned out to be superficial; until the cameras were brought out and she was ordered to turn her backside to the camera or place a bag over her head.

It had been a good day and the beach had served us well until late afternoon. We'd made full use of the small, nearby café for a light lunch and drinks, to supplement our bottles of water – relaxing the earlier commitment – to unnecessary spending. The simple pleasure of having the time and opportunity for everyone to do their own thing, whether it be reading, swimming or sunbathing, was the main reason behind our smiles. Sunbathing seemed to be the preferred choice for most, producing a lobster pink glow to their sun-starved bodies. With Factor 30 sun block plastered over every inch of my exposed skin, plus my 'pith helmet' sun hat, which threw a protecting shadow around the delicate parts of my face, neck and ears, I decided to take off for a walk along the beach, leaving the girls to cook a little more.

An hour or so later, as I walked back to join them, I could tell that the next stage of activity was being discussed and organised. Not by Lil this time; she was keeping well back from the fray. I'm sure George had offered a diplomatic word – to wind in the authoritative organising – at least for a while. The body language of each individual was quite easy to read at a couple of hundred yards, especially with the sun behind me. The more dominant characters, with heads pushed forward, articulating mainly with their arms, could almost be heard – particularly Sylvia – who is never embarrassed to be told that she has a voice like a foghorn. Carol was standing quite relaxed, not saying much, but she was close enough to the others to be involved. The discussion was obviously equable, so I started to walk more quickly, so as not to be left out of the arrangements.

'Have you got the kitty purse, Marg?' called June, when I was just a few feet away. I reached into my small leather bag to retrieve the replenished purse, feeling a deep sense of unease that its contents would soon be plundered. 'What's happening?' I said, trying not to sound peevish. It was then explained to me what had been decided (mainly by the ones with pushed forward heads).

Alice and Sally had been allocated the job of shopping at the supermarket for an alfresco evening meal. I caught a glimpse of their shopping list, which read: cooked chicken for the wimps, frying steak, salad, bread and potatoes. June and Carol were to head for the Bottle Shop, to buy the alcoholic beverages. Apparently no written list was needed for them. Lil and I had been given the job of carrying all the beach gear back to the shacks, before setting up the modest tables and chairs outside on the small patch of grassed area that was included in the territory of the accommodation.

'What about Sylvia?' I asked, intrigued to know her allotted role. This question was answered by Sylvia herself, 'I need to get back and have a shower.' I opened my mouth to respond, and then thought better of it. It had been a good day, and I didn't want to be the one to spoil it.

The simplicity of eating a meal outdoors, in the company of friends or family, is a source of great delight for me. To be in close proximity to exotic plants and colourful parrots made it even more delightful, prompting me to compete with the squawking birds and burst into song, as Lil and I manoeuvred the furniture into position.

Alice and Sally were the first to return, laden down with the edibles. After emptying her arms with a heavy sigh, Sally disappeared to the shower to wash her hair, leaving Alice in charge of the cooking – a challenge she took to heart, as she proceeded to strip away the skins of a mountain of Australia's best potatoes. There was still no sign of Silvia. Left with nothing more to do, Lil and I sat at the table sampling a piece of freshly-cut, crusty bread and a glass of juice. Suddenly, a vaguely familiar clattering sound was heard. Turning in the direction of the noise, we saw June and Carol struggling to push a full-sized, supermarket trolley over the uneven ground which led to the shacks. Intrigued, we left our relaxed position and walked the few dozen yards to meet them.

The trolley was stacked high with bottles of beer of various types and strength. Amongst this mountain of amber liquid and glass, several packs of Vodka Breezers flaunted their garish, artificial colours at us. In the far corner of the trolley, standing alone and imprisoned by the rest of the cargo, stood a lone bottle of red wine. The label on this bottle of wine displayed an origin that I'd never clapped eyes on before. I looked at Lil, but her attention was conveniently elsewhere.

This bottle of cheap, red wine was plonked down (no pun intended) in front of me and Lil with a casual announcement from June, 'I don't know if that's any good, I haven't got a clue about wine.' I was starting to feel really peevish now. Everyone else obviously got asked which vintage of light ale they would prefer, or which bright colour is your favourite Vodka Breezer, but no one thought to ask me or Lil whether white or red wine would go better with our wimpy chicken. I looked again to Lil for a little support, but she was still sitting firmly on the diplomatic fence.

The sun went down unnoticed, as we talked and munched our way through most of the food. Lil was beginning to yawn noisily, which was a clear sign that she wanted to go home, so I started to clear a space on the table, to allow for fruit and coffee. Suddenly I found several eager hands ready to help and before I realised what was happening, half of the chairs had been hurriedly carried back into their respective shacks. The penny dropped with an almighty clang when I heard Sylvia's loud voice bellow out in the direction of Alice, 'And

47

you're not coming with a face like that, you look like a battered wife.'

'I don't want to go Sylvia, mi mouth's sore and I need an early night.' Alice's meek response was made through tightly held together lips, trying hard not to disturb the healing cut, which arched from the corner of her mouth down to the bottom of her chin.

Somewhere along the line I'd missed the added arrangements of a night out on the town. But I should have guessed, when Sylvia finally decided to put in an appearance after all the chores were done. Although casually dressed, she looked as though she'd just stepped out of the hair salon. In contrast to my wild, curly mop – a legacy from swimming in the ocean – her crowning glory shone from the timely effects of washing, blow-drying, straightening and the application of the many hair products that this entailed. I suppose, after relaxing on the beach for most of the day, built-up energy was waiting to be released. I personally felt very relaxed after my long walk earlier and the two glasses of wine (which tasted quite good, after all).

'I'll stay here with Alice,' I offered.

'She's sixty-five years old, she doesn't need a babysitter.' Sylvia announced to the whole neighbourhood, as she brought in the last chair.

'I'd like to stay in and catch up on some reading,' I said, determined not to be overridden.

'Well I'm on holiday and I'm gonna have a bloody good time, 'ow about you lot?' Several heads nodded in agreement.

Out came the bling- bling, the smart bottoms and the frilly tops, worn with even more confidence, due to the deepening colour of their skin. In no time at all Alice and I were waving goodbye to four overexcited sisters, giggling like a bunch of teenagers, as they squeezed into a pre-ordered taxi.

Alice offered me one of her Vodka Breezers, which I declined, saying that the wine had been sufficient.

'Would you mind if I prop myself up on the bed to read?' I asked, taking advantage of her generous mood; after all it was her turn for the bed.

'Course I don't mind, I'm gonna 'av a good read *miself*,' she responded through tight lips.

Three lines into my book a sudden loud conversation broke into the peace and quiet of the shack. Alice had turned the television on. The large, grey, plastic box, which to my mind, was unnecessarily taking up too much valuable space, was glowing with bright, slightly fuzzy, moving images, as the sound reverberated off the walls. I glared in Alice's direction, hoping that her timid state would bow to my wishes and turn the bloody thing off. It was useless; she was sitting with her back to me at the table, her nose pressed into a magazine.

This horrendous intrusion continued for at least fifteen minutes. I read the same paragraph over and over again and still couldn't make sense of it. Using the same tone of voice I use when speaking to my two-year-old granddaughter, who quite often wants to do several things at the same time, I asked her why she needed the telly on while she was reading. She turned and looked at me, flashing what I thought was an angry snarl, before realising it was her disfigured mouth, playing tricks with the shadows. 'Oh, you never know, we might get one of those Australian soaps on soon,' she said as brightly as she could manage through closed lips. A sudden flash of inspiration hit me as I wrestled with a suitable reply.

'Did you know that we have to pay for all television viewing time?'

As light-footed as a ballerina, she was off her chair and reaching for the off button on the set, and within three seconds flat, we were plunged into silent sanity.

8

I woke up early having had a good night's rest, the only disturbance being a vague recollection of Sally coming in and trying to be quiet, but not quite succeeding. I'd had no idea of the time, because fortunately, she hadn't turned on any lights and lying in my bottom bunk, cut off the view of anything above ten inches from the floor. In the very dim light of moonshine filtered through curtains, a view of her feet and lower limbs was all I had, until she'd finally hoisted herself up into the middle bunk.

I'd taken to having my showers at the communal shower block, because unlike the shower in the shack, they were spacious and very well equipped, and rising at six in the morning, you were more than likely to have the place to yourself.

Washing away the remains of sleep under the constantly hot gushing water left me refreshingly alert and clear-minded. The shower block and its surroundings were still deserted when I stepped back into the warm morning sunshine, even though my ablutions hadn't been hurried and I'd taken time to hand wash my smalls.

Peering around the door of the nearby laundry room reminded me of the mounting load of heavy washing that needed to be attended to. This room was also well equipped, but unlike the shower block, you needed to come armed with money – or its equivalent in tokens – obtainable from the site office. The washing machines were quite economical and ideal for a heavy wash, but the dryers were proving to be an unnecessary drain on the kitty purse; and to my mind quite unnecessary, considering we were blessed with a perfect drying climate. Filled with a strong sense of determination to locate or erect a washing line and, taking advantage of the quiet, early hour, I wandered around the utilitarian areas of

51

the site. Within five minutes I found exactly what I wanted and had been given permission to use it from one of the site attendants.

Feeling very pleased with my achievement and wanting to share this pleasure I made my way back to the shack. It was deathly quiet. The curtain was pulled fully around the double bed, telling me that Alice was still fast asleep and the sliding door hiding Sally, was just as I'd left it. Not wanting to disturb this unfamiliar silence, I decided to take a walk to the supermarket and replenish our dwindling stock of milk.

Walking the short distance, along the now familiar roads, reminded me that early morning is the very best time of day, wherever you happen to be. All my senses were alert to my surroundings – which were beautiful – and the deep breaths of salt-laden air gave me a strong sense of well being.

I returned with two large bottles of semi-skimmed, knowing my choice would earn me some strange looks from one or two faces, but I was too relaxed to care. The lower fat milk is healthier and as I had been the one to put in the leg work, I should be allowed to choose. I tapped lightly on next doors shack. A few grunts later the door was opened several inches, into which I passed the milk, being careful to keep the label facing away from the taker – who happened to be Sylvia. She made another grunt which sounded like thanks, before closing the door.

'Did you wet the bed?' was Sally's morning greeting, as I let myself into our shack. I sensed her gratitude as I handed her the milk; she'd just made tea, so was aware that there wasn't enough for the cereals we'd all become used to having. Alice had been allowed in the small shower area first, so I settled down beside Sally at the table and prompted her about the 'night on the town.' The look on her face spoke volumes, but I was still eager to hear chapter and verse of where they'd spent the evening.

They'd asked the taxi driver to drop them at Brighton, a few miles along the seafront, where they'd remembered seeing lots of pavement café's on a previous bus journey. They'd thought that this day-time hive of activity would increase to buzzing by evening-time.

'Brighton in Australia is not like Brighton in England,' I interrupted, 'most of Australia's small cafés close up in the evening.'

I was stating the obvious and the look on her face implied that I should keep my mouth shut and let her tell the tale. She finished in a flurry by going on to say how they'd searched without success for a lively pub and eventually settled for a couple of beers in a quiet bar, before securing a taxi to bring them home.

Just as we'd finished clearing from breakfast, Lil arrived looking very pleased and self-satisfied. We had planned to spend several days of our three-week trip in the Blue Mountains and she had been busy at home from early morning, arranging this on our behalf. Using her persuasive bargaining skills and polished telephone manner she'd managed to secure us four days in a motel that was familiar to her, at a very good price. And what was especially good news – all our meals would be included in this very good price.

Furthermore, after hearing that we weren't over the moon at the thought of returning to the shacks after the mountain trip, she'd selected two, suitable (meaning low cost) motels on the outskirts of Sydney, for our final week.

'What I want you lot to do is check out these two motels, so that we can get one booked before we leave for the highlands, even though that's six days away.' Lil's final words on the subject held a ring of authority that showed she was back to her old self.

Two pots of tea sat in the middle of the table as the seven of us circled it in boardroom fashion, ready to arrange the next step forward – viewing the two Sydney motels. Lil's emphatic request that we check out the accommodation before committing to it, was sound advice. She didn't know either place and wasn't about to fall into a trap of blame, especially after the moans and groans that resulted from her choice of the shacks. We were all aware that money – or should I say the lack of it – was more of a problem to some than it was to others, and although we have always been generous in the sharing department, we are also fiercely independent about paying our own way. Bearing this in mind, it was a relief to know that we could now pay up for the remainder of the trip's accommodation, giving us a better indication of the money left for pleasure spending.

'We can't all fit in my car, so I'll take one of you from each cabin,' suggested Lil, who had taken the chair, so to speak, in the absence of any other forthcoming, sensible suggestions. Sylvia, who was quickly getting fed up with all this boardroom meeting malarkey said, 'June can go from our lot, she's sensible.' Alice and Sally both looked at me. I'd been chosen, not necessarily because they thought I was the most sensible, they just wanted to get down to the beach, to work on their respective suntans.

'Wow! look at the size of this family room,' enthused Lil, as we wandered around the luxurious, three-roomed suite.

'It's only got one bathroom and it hasn't got six independent beds; why can't we just rent two, three-bedded rooms?' I said, knowing that I was deflating her mood.

'I agree,' said June, 'one bathroom will be a nightmare; why can't we rent two rooms?'

'Not available and too expensive,' was the prompt reply. We drove off to the second location, which was just down the road.

What was offered here for the same amount of money were two, tacky rooms, each furnished with three beds, but not much else apart from a small annexed shower room. No cooking facilities, except for the obligatory electric kettle and no table or chairs. I was already missing the shacks, with all the taken for granted facilities. June, with a pragmatic air, said, 'It's only for a week. I think we should take this one. What do you think, Lil?' Her eyes moved slowly around the dowdy space, and as if thinking aloud said, 'Well, you wouldn't get George to stay here,' then added, 'I don't want to influence, it's up to you.' No decision was made.

As the three of us pulled into the usual parking space at the camp site, it was obvious that beach frolicking was off the menu for the rest of today. Billowing, grey clouds had materialised from all directions, completely covering the azure blue sky we had started to take for granted. An unwelcome chilly breeze whipped around our bare legs as we quickly headed for the shelter of the shacks.

'I don't do walking,' is a constantly used phrase of Sylvia's. She even has it printed on a tee shirt to reiterate the fact. But the constant exercise – voluntarily taken or not – over the last few days, coupled with fresh, sea air and sunshine, was loosening our aging joints and toning our bodies, helping us to feel more lithe and energetic. A quick sandwich, followed by a long walk, was unanimously decided upon. I couldn't think of a better way to spend the afternoon.

We crossed the beach road, turning right instead of our customary left. Dolls Point was way off in the distance and although no one actually voiced that this was our destination, we were drawn towards it, as we talked and stopped from time to time, allowing the slower members of the group to catch up.

Dotted along the shoreline road were a mixture of individually designed houses; and there was no denying that without exception, they were built for the mega-rich. Ultra large balconies – protected from sea breezes by vast sheets of plate glass and steel – were on clear view as we craned our necks to evaluate the adjoining gardens and outdoor statuary. Seeing these beautiful properties reminded me of a childhood game I used to indulge in, on my long walk home from school. I'd choose a number from one to ten, and then count off the houses until I reached that number, pretending that's where I lived. It was a novelty to share this naive little game with my sisters and it was interesting to see how our tastes varied when it came to the perfect dream home – because a fair amount of imaginary swapping took place. As a child I wasn't so fussy, almost any number presented a house looking more prestigious than our humble dwelling.

As Dolls Point got closer, the wind was more keenly felt and so was the need for refreshments. Lil suddenly shot off ahead and as she was enveloped into the noisy, blustering wind, 'I know... coffee...' were the only distinct words we heard. We followed in the same direction for about twenty minutes, frustrated at not being able to see her ahead and concerned about the ever increasing gap behind. The slower walkers were oblivious to what was happening. Sally and I put on a spurt leaving June to drop back and inform the other three.

Eventually, we came upon a large boat that had been tastefully converted into a café. There were clear signs indicating that it was open, but no sign of Lil. In fact the place was empty of customers. Without giving her any choice, I left Sally sitting at the nearest table, whilst I dashed to the loo. I'd been bursting to go for ages. No more than two minutes had passed but I returned to find the eager café owner, already hovering with her notepad, and Sally looking very sheepish. I sat down and Sally shot off, almost dragging her chair with her as she too, needed to empty her bladder. The café owner, a middle-aged woman of medium build and stern expression, positioned herself between my chair and the café exit. She was armed with her notepad and pen.

I said, quite truthfully, 'There are seven of us, do you mind if we wait a few minutes for the others to catch up?' My words brought a smile to her face and a bolt of energy to her body as she dragged a heavy table alongside and proceeded to set up for seven, humming as she worked.

Sally returned, looking even more embarrassed, as she watched the café owner's efforts and her broadening smile, when she said, 'I'll just get the list of today's Specials.' As soon as she disappeared from view, we scurried off that boat like thieves in the night.

Back on the ocean road we turned to the sound of familiar voices. The slower walkers had caught up and were heading for the welcome sign of the boat café. We grabbed them just in time to prevent a rerun of our antics, knowing that they all needed the loo. Another twenty minutes of walking produced no sign of Lil, or another café. We began to wonder if she'd been blown off the point into the swirling waters below and

Sylvia began to wonder how long she could keep her knickers dry.

'Here she comes,' said Carol, spying Lil sauntering towards us with a relaxed, unconcerned air. We marched forward while she stood still, but before we were allowed to catch up completely she turned tail and indicated for us to follow. Determined not to loose her again we caught up as she rounded the point and entered a swimming pool café. This had been Lils preferred choice all along, and none of us were surprised when the café assistant greeted Lil with a 'Back again?' welcome. She was well and truly in the dog house, especially as the choice of fare here was very limited, compared to the boat café. 'The coffee's very good,' she said feebly.

'Sod the coffee, we drink tea!' Sylvia blurted out, as she shot off to the toilet block.

The mood was more sullen as we walked back. However, the atmosphere brightened when we came upon a huge cannon; placed to commemorate an early battle at sea. Lil whipped out her camera and no orders were necessary as we clambered on and sat astride the massive metal tube. Sylvia sat in front position – skirt hitched up so much that her knickers were clearly on view. I suppose it could have been worse: if she'd wet them back there, she wouldn't have had any on!

The air in the cabin was an exotic mix of three different brands of perfume, a dash of hairspray and a slight undertone of the food we'd consumed earlier; which was the remains of yesterday's alfresco meal.

Sally had changed tops at least four times, convincing me that this was her way of justifying the huge pile that she'd brought. Alice's attention was absorbed in her countless strands of bling-bling; which she kept hung over a convenient hook at the side of the double bed, only inches from the face of whoever happened to be sleeping there. I watched intrigued, as she very carefully lay one after another over her head; deciding which best complimented her clothes, but didn't clash with the healing bruises that now had soft patches of yellow within the blue. I was ready; had been for ages; but was in no hurry to leave. We were going to the local RSL club just a ten-minute walk away. Live music was promised on the display board and being Friday night – an unwritten rule worldwide – meant it would be busy, with an atmosphere that had been denied us since we'd arrived on Australian soil. It also meant lots of drinking – and I was the weakling in this department – so I was happy to diminish the time doing it. Lil was spending this evening with George, and who could blame her, they hadn't shared much time together during the last week.

Alice secured a table directly in front of the area allocated for the band, which hadn't yet set up. I handed June the kitty purse with my order of white wine and soda hoping it would last me half the evening. We all felt beautiful, and of course, what you feel is what you are. Bright, smiling faces: sun kissed, then kissed a little more with delicate shades of make up, to enhance – or in Alice's case, disguise – our main features. We were dressed for dancing and all the colours of the rainbow, highlighted with touches of gold or silver, would be gyrated, twirled or shaken tonight.

It had been a really good night, and later as I lay in the middle bunk with Alice safely rolled into the bottom one and Sally playing the Queen of Sheba in the big bed, I relived the happiness of it.

The lead singer of the band was a middle-aged chap, short in stature, but in possession of a very powerful voice. Everyone in the crowded room – including the very old – was inspired, as he revived perfectly, songs from the sixties, seventies and eighties. The pleasure he'd enjoyed from sharing his talents was undeniable, and in return, we all responded with an energy that was sustained throughout the evening – freshened from time to time with beer or white wine and soda.

We'd all been reluctant to leave, wanting to hang on to the happy abandon – found in dancing – but the music was finished. The poor chap had given his all, satisfying our shouts for more, many times, but eventually he'd turned his back on our pleading faces and started to dismantle the microphone.

Walking back to the shacks, still wrapped in the afterglow of the good time we'd all had, I sensed a bond building between us, and the strengthening of this bond was the main reason I was here in Australia. Again, I silently renewed the vow, to make the most of this precious time together.

'Come on lazy bones, time you were up, it's Rovers' Day,' Sally shouted from the other side of the closed, sliding door, which annoyingly interrupted my concentration. With my ear conveniently close to the wall, I'd been listening to Sylvia's side of a conversation that she was having with her husband. This told me two things: she had remedied the mobile phone problem and June and Carol must also be awake – no one could sleep through that noise – especially when personal details were offered, loud and clear. The whole neighbourhood learned that the imminently expected birth of her grandchild hadn't yet happened.

'Come on you Blues,' sang out Sally, as she tinkled a teaspoon provocatively in a mug of tea, enticing me out of bed. I felt groggy from too much sleep and too much alcohol, even though I'd consumed less than half anyone else. How do they do it and still feel so bright the next morning?

I slid open the partition door and my eyes fell on a sea of blue and white paper that filled every inch of the table and chairs, except the one where Alice sat studiously working.

'Come over 'ere, Marg, I need yer 'ed.' My brain actually hurt, trying to understand what she meant, and it was only the gormless look on my face that prompted her to enlarge on the request.

'Come 'ere, I need to try this on your 'ed, to make sure it fits.'

She held out a long tube of blue and white crepe paper, pinched in, halfway along its length, with one half cut into tassels.

'I'm not wearing that!' I protested loudly as Sally's head swung round, revealing a look of near apoplexy, then shock, then rage, all in two seconds flat.

'Yes, you are lady and you're wearing the spare football shirt I struggled to squeeze into my suitcase for you. Rovers are playing tonight, and we'll all be dressed for it as we watch them on the big screen, Lil's sorting it today.'

It was pretty obvious that breakfast was of no consequence at this point in time, so after silently drinking the tea that had been grudgingly shoved into my hand, I gathered my clothes and toilet bag, to head for the shower block.

'Where are you going?' mumbled Alice, as she struggled to speak with at least four straight pins in her mouth – adding a spiky-punk effect to the much diminished bruising.

'I'm going to have a shower seeing as you're so busy,' I answered in a good natured voice, which surprised me because I was seething inside.

'We're all going be busy, 'ere blow them up,' Alice mumbled again, with even more pins in her mouth. Fearing that she might swallow them whilst struggling to speak, I reluctantly abandoned my toilet bag and towel, and looked aghast at the two, plastic, inflatable trophies that she'd thrown at me.

'Margaret, you should be proud that Rovers have got this far. We're proud and we want to show our support,' said Sally, in a soft pacifying tone.

'Yes, but here in Australia, I'm sure no one will have even heard of Blackburn Rovers,' I replied, in an even softer tone, because my head was now spinning from lack of oxygen after inflating the first of the two monstrosities.

'Well they will after tonight, because we'll raise the roof with our cheering,' they both shouted in unison, causing me to jump in fright and nearly lose the precarious balance I held on the edge of the bed – the only space I could find to perform this doleful task. I decided it was safer to keep my mouth clamped around the teat of the foul-tasting, plastic obscenity, and not say another word.

Struggling to produce enough breath to inflate the two, tacky, representations of… God knows what, tipped my low morale into full blown resentment. I felt like the captive slave of a strange tribe of women, who were gearing up in full battle dress for an approaching war dance. I'd already fallen into the trap of agreeing to arrive at Sydney Airport wearing a rugby shirt that displayed the England team's achievement of 2002. I find it hard to believe now that I did it. In fact I can't believe that I spent over twenty pounds on a tee shirt that I'll never wear again. Apart from the waste of money, the whole idea of arriving in another man's country and visually proclaiming 'we' are better than 'you' just didn't feel right. Who in their right mind would want to antagonise the Australians? They're a happy-go-lucky, warm and welcoming people.

The thought of antagonising jolted me back to the present. Not wanting to sever the delicate bond that had started to grow between us, I decided to play along once again, thankful that it would only last for one day. June is even more fanatical than Alice and Sally when it comes to the following of Blackburn Rovers; providing I'm sure, a necessary link between the home and family she'd moved away from years ago. Sylvia, on the other hand, is definitely not a football fan, but even she had been press-ganged into joining the tribe, without any obvious fuss. I wasn't sure of Carol's position when it came to kicking a ball around, but I know she would join in good naturedly to anything, so long as we were all together. Lil and George were obviously happy to run with it, by organising the viewing venue. I was the miserable bugger in the spotlight today.

63

I helped tie the air-fattened trophies to the outside of each cabin, alongside banners proclaiming the Rover's past glories. People walked by looking amused or confused and some even intrigued enough to ask questions, the delight on my sister's faces when responding enlarged the guilt I was starting to feel.

Feeling replete from a my breakfast and refreshed from a vigorous shower, I decided to allow my sisters complete freedom to enjoy their fanaticism, without my constant carping. I'd go for a long walk and indulge in a little retail therapy to cheer myself up.

I'd intended to walk to my chosen destination of Brighton-le-Sands, using the beach road that ran parallel to the coast. This road was interspersed every mile or so by parkland and gardens, allowing the stroller or power-walker interludes of shade, whilst still being able to enjoy the benefits of the ocean. But the partnership of sun on water provided such an evocative spectacle of diamond-studded movement, that I decided to leave the coast road to the keep fitters and meld into the magic by going barefoot along the water's edge.

I encountered four fishermen on my watery journey, all of them of Greek origin. They were no doubt obeying a deep instinct that had run through the blood of their race for countless generations. Gazing out across the sparkling water, enticing edible sea life onto their lines, probably evoked strong memories of the tranquil islands of their homeland. Each smiled contentedly when I asked them if they'd caught anything, even though the answer from all four, was a shake of the head.

About a mile away from Brighton-le-Sands, I was suddenly stopped in my tracks by a huge pile of boulders strategically positioned to help prevent sand erosion, which was evident at this end of the long beach. I was faced with the choice of scrambling over them to locate the next exit onto the coast road, or backtrack the five-hundred yards or so to the previous exit. Looking again at the tonnes of jagged rock ahead of me and the blazing sun above me, I reluctantly turned around to retrace my steps, feeling irritated at my lack of observation as to what was happening ahead. I'd been lost in deep thoughts of how it must feel to reside in another man's country; a subject too close to home, not to be given the occasional airing. Barry and I had been enjoying winter holidays on the Canary Island of Lanzarote for some time. The year round warm climate, coupled with the laid-back Spanish culture, had seduced Barry into wanting to move there lock, stock and barrel. I was the sticking point.

Back tracking to the previous exit to the coast road proved to be the better decision. Not only was there a very welcome toilet block – equipped with a water fountain to replenish my almost empty water bottle – but directly opposite, across the busy main road, was just what I had set out to find: a beach and surfers retail outlet. Racks and racks of brightly coloured merchandise were positioned on the pavement to tempt the passing public and allow them time to browse, without the watchful eye of an over-zealous assistant putting them off.

I'd brought two pairs of shorts with me to Australia, one black and the other white, but I was in the mood for wearing a bit more colour. None of my sisters were shy about wearing the most vivid and vibrant of colours, no matter what the occasion, and remembering Carol's lovely sunshine yellow outfit of the night before – and how she'd looked twenty years younger than her actual age – fuelled my determination to be a little more adventurous.

Shorts in every colour of the rainbow were hanging along one rail. Blue was definitely out of the question; I didn't want the tribe thinking that I'd been converted. I settled on a colour at the opposite end of the colour spectrum, which I love. A well designed, lightweight pair in bright orange, with side panels of white and pink. They fitted perfectly, and an end of season discount of 30% put a skip in my step as I walked back barefoot along the sea shore to join the rest of the tribe.

I could see everyone, including Lil and George, sitting on the veranda of the beach café as I strolled along the last stretch of sand. Seeing them all eating brought to mind a hunger that hadn't been apparent until now. After pulling a chair over to join them, and ordering a light lunch, I showed them the colourful content of my carrier bag. Everyone agreed that I'd made a good choice and June promptly offered me an orange top which matched the shorts perfectly. Lil said she also had an orange top, which would look better on me than her. I was beginning to feel, well and truly 'tangoed'.

'This food is really good,' said Sylvia as she licked her fingers. She was sitting opposite me on a table for eight, at Lil and George's favourite Indian restaurant in Beverly Hills. It was a regular Saturday evening haunt of theirs, and although the place was extremely busy, the owner had kept a large table in reserve, knowing that they might want to bring along their visiting relatives. Carol, Sylvia and myself were delighted to have been brought along, especially as the dishes were refreshingly different from the Indian cuisine back home. We had a very pleasurable time, dipping into each others choices, to compare the various exotic flavours.

June, Sally and Alice had gone ahead to the club; where we would later watch the match. We had all driven up there earlier in the afternoon, in Lil and George's cars, just to make absolutely sure that this particular match would in fact be available on the large screen. It was. Not content with this assurance, the three fanatics insisted on dining at the club – in order to give them ample opportunity to secure a large table, close enough to the big screen.

'Do you realise that these hats could be a fire hazard?' I grumbled, as I stood in front of the large mirror, in the Ladies Room of the club.

'Why, do you think your brain's going to get over excited, and burst into flames?' answered Sally, with a cheeky grin on her face, as she whipped out an oversized football shirt from her bag. It was reluctantly slipped on over my more glamorous outfit and, as I donned the tasselled, paper hat, I made a mental note to stay well clear of any smokers.

Rovers lost three nil to Arsenal, which was very disappointing, but not as disappointing as watching the gradual deflating of the earlier exuberant mood of my sisters. In complete contrast, George was beaming like a Cheshire cat. He'd had a very enjoyable evening and the Rovers losing seemed to have heightened his enjoyment, even though he too was wearing a blue and white tasselled-hat.

It was getting quite late and the effect of the long walk earlier, the satisfying meal and too much shouting and hollering, was taking its toll. To help put a smile on at least Alice's face, I asked her if she wanted to share the double bed. A strange request I know, but it was my rightful turn again, and I felt certain that even her loud snoring wouldn't keep me awake tonight. Plus, Rovers losing, and having to

67

sleep in the fated middle bunk, was too much to ask of any sixty-five-year-old sister.

'Yes please,' was her simple response.

'There is a proviso,' I added. She frowned slightly, showing me that she didn't have a clue what I was talking about.

Lil had offered earlier to give a lift home to three of us, before returning to drive George home. He had drunk too much to drive his own car, which would be left overnight in the car park. This, she said, would give him a chance for a little more intoxication in the company of the remaining three sisters. I was first in line for the offered lift, and my proviso to Alice, was that she joined me. I didn't mind her sharing the bed – there was more than enough room for us both – but I did object to being disturbed once I was in a deep sleep. She agreed, and Sylvia agreed to be the third passenger, which really surprised me. She then mentioned something about phoning home before it got too late, which diminished any hopes of me getting to sleep straight away.

10

The usual Sunday morning sounds of back home – church bells, mingled with the soft cooing melody of wood pigeons – were replaced with the harsh, raucous noise of parrots arguing for territory. Alice was still fast asleep; her nose only two inches away from her hanging pile of shining metal. The curtain was pulled fully around the double bed, without the slightest chink visible. I paid particular attention to its closure, in anticipation of Sally coming in late and turning the light on whilst humming the Rover's signature tune, which seemed to have got well and truly stuck in one of her mental grooves. I'd heard nothing, and the undisturbed curtain showed that neither me nor Alice had needed to use the loo in the night; which was very unusual.

It felt early, but knowing that I wouldn't be able to get any more sleep, and amazed that anyone else could with the deafening noise outside, I got up and filled the kettle, in the hope that this would bring one or other of my sisters to the edge of wakefulness.

Sally was first to take the bait, emerging from the sliding door and reaching for the steaming mug of tea as if her life depended on it. I gave her a chance to have several gulps of the elixir, guessing by the look on her face she wasn't capable of a lucid conversation yet. My silent patience to hear the detail of how their evening had ended was suddenly interrupted by Alice, peering through the double bed curtain and saying in a voice as harsh as the parrots outside, 'What time did you get in last night lady?'

It transpired that after a couple more drinks with George, and before wishing him and Lil goodnight, June had asked at the bar for a taxi to be ordered. She was advised to stand outside the club and hail one down. The adviser went on to say that on a Saturday night its every man for himself and

69

most of the taxis would be in the heart of Sydney making big bucks. Feeling confident that one was bound to pass their way, they waited at the three-way junction across from the club. Three pairs of eyes split between the three possibilities.

They waited, apparently without success, for fifty-five minutes. The truth is, they could have walked home in that time, but the late hour and the unfamiliar area made them too nervous to attempt it. Eventually, worry and desperation sent June back into the empty club, where she relayed their plight to a security guard who was systematically locking all the doors. After telling June to hang on, he disappeared briefly and returned with the driver of the clubs service minibus – free transport for pensioners to and from the club – provided they lived within the clubs catchment area. The driver agreed to give them a lift home, as long as they covered the cost of the petrol because Ramsgate was out of the free zone.

At this point Sally's face brightened as she recalled the relief she'd felt at this unexpected offer of help.

'I could have flung my arms around him and offered three times the cost of the petrol,' she said smiling. Alarm bells started to clang in my head, as a mental image of three women flinging their arms and their money at a perfect stranger, made me wonder where this was leading.

The smile disappeared from Sally's face as she continued to explain that June had climbed in the front passenger seat alongside the driver.

'Why did she do that,' I interrupted, 'a minibus has got plenty of seats?' Sally gave me a look that implied – keep your mouth shut and you'll soon find out – before continuing to explain that June needed to guide him to the shacks when they reached Ramsgate. As June climbed in beside him, the driver handed her a map book, helpfully opened at the

70

appropriate page, telling her that he was a foreigner to the world outside his usual catchment area.

Without realizing what she was doing, Sally lifted her empty tea mug to her lips, and when nothing passed between the mug and her lips her face took on the worried, haunted look she'd had prior to sitting down at the table. I promptly filled up her mug with the remains of the teapot. Alice and I, and even the parrots, were poised in silence, waiting to hear what happened next.

After two hefty gulps she continued. Apparrently June, not being a driver herself, was a little bit panicked at being given responsibility of co-driver, especially after looking over the map page and saying that she couldn't read it because it was printed in a foreign language. At this point the driver snatched it from her, studied it for a moment, and then said – in broken, pigeon, English – 'Stupid, you look at it upside down.' No one laughed, they hadn't liked the way he'd aggressively grabbed the book, then plonked it down hard in her lap the right way up. Feeling even more panicked, June attempted to make sense of all the fine, squiggly lines that led to the word Ramsgate.

Sally picked up her mug to swallow its remains; her nervous gulps punctuating the palpable silence. Alice looked all set to nudge her back into action after the lengthy pause, but my hand on her arm and the glaring look on my face, stopped her in her impatient tracks.

Eventually, in a lowered voice, she continued by saying that she remembered being driven down the same road, over and over again. They drove over the river bridge twice, and all three women knew that crossing the river was unnecessary, notching up their nervousness even more. Her voice started to break up as she recalled the fear of a kidnap attempt, thinking all the back doubling on the roads was a smoke screen to confuse them. It was tempting to interrupt again at this point with a humorous pun, but the serious look on her face caused me to hold my tongue.

A sudden knocking on the cabin door made all three of us jump. Alice, being the closest, shot off her seat and accosted the closed door with a ferocious, hissing sound that was obviously understood by the knocker, because Sylvia's confused voice bellowed in return, 'It's me!'

'Well bugger off for ten minutes,' hissed Alice, before returning to her seat and folding her arms, reminding me of Mum when she was in a bad mood.

This interruption seemed to have had a profound effect on Sally and her story. She continued more light-heartedly, saying that at last they spotted a sign to Ramsgate, and with an added touch of bravado, concluded, 'It took more than a bloody hour and twenty minutes to get home, when really it should have taken less than fifteen minutes.'

'I hope you flung your arms around him for a good night kiss, along with the extra large tip,' I said amused, but her blank stare told me that this was not appreciated.

The knocking returned, louder and more persistent, Sylvia was in no mood for a second rebuff.

'Sally was telling us about the bad experience of last night,' I offered, as I let her in, hoping to stall a verbal attack on Alice.

'Carol told me all about it, stupid buggers,' was her only reference to the whole sorry incident.

'We've decided to go and have a proper Sunday breakfast in the café, are you coming?' asked Sylvia, forcing the focus of attention away from last night. Sally's eyes wandered over the almost-empty packet of cereals, the last banana – from a bunch devoid of flavour, even after ripening for days – and the container of pumpkin seeds that had made her gums so sore she'd had to use Alice's soothing mouth gel.

'Count me in,' she said forcefully, showing no sign of her earlier nervousness.

'And me,' said Alice. All eyes turned on me expectantly.

'Yes I'll come, it's Sunday,' I said, leaving a confounded look on all their faces.

The six of us wandered leisurely into the small café that was situated within a ten minute walk to the shacks. A middle-aged man, reading his newspaper, was the only other customer. A notice on the counter informed us to place our orders at the bar prior to finding a seat. I needed to pop next door to the newsagents for stamps and a note book, so I left the girls, saying, 'I'll have the same as you lot except no fried bread, no sausages and no baked beans; in fact, egg and bacon with brown toast will be fine.'

My timing was perfect. The waitress was just unloading the large tray of breakfasts onto the table. But my sisters' choice of table was far from perfect. The poor chap who had been quietly reading his newspaper was now hemmed into a corner. The table next to him and the table in front of him had been placed together (by one of our lot), to allow enough surface space for five and a half large, English breakfasts. As if this wasn't bad enough, Sylvia's mouth was directly in line with his right ear.

'Why did you sit here?' I whispered across the table, to anyone that would listen.

'Why, what's wrong with it?' answered Sylvia – unfortunately not in a whisper.

'The place is empty and that poor chap is trying to read his paper, lets move down a few tables,' I said, sharpening the whisper to a hiss in order to gain as strong an impact, as Alice had done earlier.

'You must be joking! I'm not moving all this lot, if he doesn't like it, let him move;' said Sylvia, stabbing her sausage and shoving one end of it in her mouth. I looked around the table for the slightest hint of support, but they were all too engrossed in their food. All due credit to the poor chap, instead of gathering up his paper and retreating to a more peaceful area, he turned his offended ear towards the wall, flicked his newspaper aggressively and continued with his Sunday morning ritual – his tight-line lips, exaggerating the defiant look on his face.

The breakfast was delicious and enjoyed by us all, and apart from the odd appreciative word and lots of lip smacking, a tentative coexistence prevailed in the café.

'We'll need to top this up again, girls,' I said, as I almost emptied the kitty purse to pay for the breakfasts. The plates had been cleared and the bill had arrived with a fresh pot of tea. We each started to dip into our own purses for $50 to replenish the communal one. June, understandably, deducted the personal money she had spent on taxis from her levy. This, for some strange reason made Sylvia really agitated.

'Put the full money in, and then take out what it owes you, that keeps it fair and less confusing,' she aimed at June in a louder voice than usual to emphasise her point. I'm no mathematical genius, but I'd come across far more financially challenging problems than this when sharing out the proceeds from carol singing as a seven-year-old. According to the content of the interruptions from the rest of the table, everyone else was just as nonplussed at Sylvia's flawed persistent reasoning. June, feeling that her honesty and integrity were being brought into question, defended her honour by joining Sylvia in a stand-up, verbal battle.

74

As the slanging match continued, the poor chap got more and more agitated. The thick, broadsheet newspaper was flicked repeatedly in such a way to cause maximum paper noise. And, when this failed to have any effect, I began to wonder if he might be tempted into rolling it up and using it as a weapon to restore peace and quiet. I felt embarrassed, and not only because of this lone reader. The owners of the café were looking seriously worried that maybe the filled teapot, a goodwill gesture for our custom, might suddenly fly through the air.

'I think we should do this in private,' I said calmly but forcefully, taking the money – which included a generous tip – and the full teapot, to the payment desk. I apologised to the owners before walking out of the café, hoping they would all follow. They did.

La Parouse was typical of any beauty spot the world over, in as much as hoards of families visited it on a sunny, Sunday afternoon. What gave this site an added bonus, especially in a hot, dry climate like Australia, were the lush, green, softly-sloping hills that overlooked the clear, blue ocean. It was perfect for picnickers.

We had been brought out here on our arrival day to be shown, fleetingly, one of the obvious treasures of the Sydney city-dweller. But unfortunately, the grogginess of jetlag reigned supreme. I did remember Lil giving a running commentary on the fortification structure – which stood proudly nearby – but for the life of me, I couldn't remember the history attached to it. This second visit, again chauffer-driven by Lil and George, held the promise of a much more pleasant experience.

A double parking space was located for the cars, before carrying our bags to a lovely vantage point where we laid down our base camp in the form of beach towels. We were now free to come and go and explore these beautiful surroundings.

'Who wants an ice-cream?' asked Carol, as I was about to reach for my camera, and she was about to reach for her purse.

'No, Carol, use this,' and I threw her the kitty purse, which was nice and fat from the mornings top-up. After placing our order, I lazily sat with George, allowing everyone else to dash to the ice-cream van; giggling excitedly, like a bunch of children. It was good to have some time to talk with George; he had a calming, balancing effect on us, which wasn't easy to explain.

After about an hour restlessness started to develop and a diversion was sought from just sitting and looking at the views. A short distance away an Aboriginal family had set up a stall selling hand-made boomerangs. The head of this family; a short, white-haired man in his later years, was also giving demonstrations on how they should be thrown. This site was perfect for giving demonstrations safely, plus he had the attention of hundreds of people as prospective customers – including six of us. I had already decided on taking back a boomerang – a present for my son Leigh – and although there is no shortage of shops selling them, I preferred to buy one from an Aboriginal who had actually made it himself. So I was more than happy to leave George on watch duty at base camp, and follow the rest of the gang.

Within a few seconds of running my eyes along the neatly hung rows of multicoloured boomerangs, I saw the one I wanted. It was a beautiful, two-tone, hardwood specimen, with the image of a leaping fish expertly carved into the broad arc of its crescent. I snatched it from the rack and held it tightly; knowing from long experience, there may be stronger hands to take it from me.

'Ooh! Can I look at that one, Marg?' asked Alice, intrigued at why I should choose one so quickly, when there were still many more to see. I held it in front of her face, but still kept a firm grip on one end. My grip tightened as Sylvia said, 'I saw that one, I was just coming to have a better look.' Then she plucked it from my hand as deftly as an eagle, swooping on an injured baby rabbit.

'Sylvia, that's the one that I want! Leigh's a Piscean and he loves carved, exotic wood; it's just perfect for him,' I whined, hating the sound of my voice. She glanced at me briefly, then after scrutinising the price, handed it back.

'Don't get your knickers in a twist, I'm looking for a bargain.'

I'd found the price to be more than fair and as I paid the head of the family, he added to the satisfaction by telling me that this particular boomerang was made by himself. A short, stubby index finger, pointed to his almost invisible signature.

Secure in the ownership of my prize, I was able to take a step back and join Lil, who had no desire to purchase boomerangs, or any other of the Aboriginal crafts that were an adjunct to this cottage industry. We sat on a nearby tree stump watching the antics of the other five, as they systematically checked the price, before appraising every article on sale. When they each had an armful of goodies, they moved as one unit into the queue for paying and even at this distance – which was well out of earshot – you could see from their body language that they were preparing to cajole and bargain for the best possible price, using the collective amount of purchases as their main bargaining chip.

The head of the Aboriginal family possessed the broadest of smiles, and his eyes portrayed a peace and happiness that we all long for but seldom find, nevertheless, he was no pushover. Unlike the poor chap reading his paper at breakfast, this shorter-than-average man harboured no fear or agitation when surrounded by a crowd of braying women demanding a good deal. He charmed them, and in return, they charmed him; each side coming away from the transaction holding a satisfaction laced with love and good will. Kisses were exchanged and photographs were taken, to revive the memory of it in later years.

'Who am I taking?' asked George looking in Lil's direction – not necessarily for her response as an expert organiser – but more to get everyone motivated and into the cars before a deluge of picnickers decided to follow suit and clog up the roads. His strategy worked. Alice and Sylvia immediately jumped into his large, executive car, with an agility that belied their large bodies. Carol looked over to the rest of us for a sign that read 'yes you can travel back the way you came' the third passenger in George's posh car. I always travelled in the front passenger seat of Lil's small saloon. Apart from understanding the quirky air-con system, which I worked manually as we drove along, the back seat passengers – who on this occasion were Sally and June, neither of whom could drive – felt somehow safer, away from the controls.

George had been folding the towels away, when we returned to base camp loaded down with armfuls of boomerangs. He'd mentioned earlier that there was a good eating place on the way back, and it was pretty obvious that satisfying his hunger was preferable to staying here any longer. His patience was tried a little when at least four of us had said we needed to use the loo.

'We'll get this lot back to the car first,' he'd said, eyeing up the mountain of stuff we'd just purchased and no doubt wondering if his car's suspension was up to the job. His patience was tried even more when Lil reminded him that we hadn't yet seen the snake demonstrations.

'Mum and Dad really enjoyed seeing that,' she'd enthused. George hadn't replied; his mouth just pressed into a thin line as he'd gathered up all the towels and marched back to the car, leaving us to bring the rest.

As luck would have it, (for George that is) the crowds were so dense around the snake handler, it was impossible to see anything. After queuing to use the toilets we made our way back to the cars, where George stood leaning against the bonnet, straight-faced and arms folded.

'Smith's,' is a long established, popular fish retail business. Its popularity, no doubt enlarged, by the added bonus of having your choice of fish or shellfish expertly cooked while you wait and served with a choice of salad or chips. Its premises are split between two sides of a very busy dual carriageway, allowing travellers from either direction the ease of pulling in and satisfying their hunger.

George pulled in, on the homeward bound side of the road. Lil, always eager to improve our lot, managed – with a little nifty, death-defying driving – to arrive on the opposite side of the dual carriageway. She explained that this side was more pleasant for eating, because of a wide, grass verge and picnic tables. George, obviously not caring about these finer points, had disregarded her earlier mention of it in favour of his growling stomach, and assumed she would follow him and stop on the easiest side.

As we looked across the wide expanse of concrete lanes filled with the fast moving blur of coloured metal, we could just make out George's outline, a bag of food in one hand, while the other frantically beckoned us across. Lil wasn't happy. The four of us held hands and gambled with our lives, to cross the road on foot.

'What were ya doin' over there?' George asked, his Geordie accent even harder to understand, due to the mouthful of oysters. It was Lil's turn to remain silent, as her lips pressed in a tight thin line encouraging George's smile to develop into an enormous grin, as he popped a couple of chips into it.

The vast selection of fish and shellfish, made choosing difficult. The portions were so large that three people could just about share; as was the case with Alice, Sylvia and Carol. George was already halfway through his choice, so there was no sharing to be had there. The four late arrivals would have to split into two sharing couples, complicating the choosing even more. I grabbed Lil's arm, knowing that her eating habits were far more adventurous than the other two. After a short deliberation we decided on the 'Special Five Fish Variety', which included squid, salad and chips, as well as a medley of succulent pieces of white fish.

The food was absolutely wonderful. It was a pity that we had to stand and eat it on the narrow verge of the slip road. Lil was uncharacteristically quiet as the rest of us threw our leftovers high into the air, for the feeding, acrobatic seagulls. I jokingly reminded her of the last meal we'd eaten in the company of seagulls, saying that maybe it was a good thing that we couldn't sit down.

'It'll take ages to cross that road and drive back round to here. I'll see you back at the cabins,' Lil shouted to George over the noise of the traffic, which had increased steadily over the last hour. Again, the four of us took our lives in our hands as we loped across the dual carriageway, one lane at a time.

'That's an interesting building,' I said, pointing to a large, well-designed, waterside property a few yards to our right. Lil was unlocking her car, but as she turned to where I was pointing she relocked it and wandered over to the building and naturally we followed.

'This is one of our favourite restaurants,' she said almost to herself, as a smile creased the thoughtful look on her face.

'Maybe we could get a coffee here?' I said, feeling the need for a warm drink to help digest the heavy meal. The glint in her eye and the broadening grin on her face told me she was thinking the same thing.

We sought out a table for four on the open, waterfront terrace, making sure we were as far away from the other patrons as possible. We were definitely underdressed. Only a third of the tables were occupied – lingerers from a late afternoon meal. But all were exquisitely dressed in their designer label, Sunday best. In comparison, we looked like something the cat had dragged in; wearing casual shorts and tee shirts – soiled from the hours of romping around the grassy slopes. We were also emitting a strong smell of fish and chips.

Lil shot off into the cool interior of the prestigious building to order four coffees. 'I'd prefer a beer,' said June, as Lil disappeared from view.

'So would I. The salty chips have made me thirsty,' said Sally, smacking her lips to emphasise her need.

'Well why didn't you say?' I hissed, feeling a strong need to be discrete, but still get my point over in Alice-like fashion.

'Because she never asked,' they said in unison.

'June, go in and catch her before it's too late,' I hissed more gently, not wanting any bad vibes to develop between us; it was embarrassing enough feeling out of place.

June and Lil returned to the table, satisfied that the changed order was being filled. I arrived back from the ladies – my hands and face scrubbed and smelling of soap – allowing me a modicum of respectability. Relaxing into the comfortable chairs we gazed across the sunlit water with a sigh of appreciation.

Our pleasurable relaxation was suddenly interrupted by an immaculately dressed waitress; a worried look creasing her lovely flawless face.

'I'm awfully sorry,' she began, in perfect Queen's English, 'I can't serve you alcohol if you're not dining.'

All eyes turned on Lil. Lil's eyes turned on June, the one guilty of upsetting the prearranged apple-cart by wanting beer instead of a civilised cup of coffee.

'We've already eaten,' responded Lil, as if the waitress couldn't detect that from the smell that still permeated the air around our table.

'I'm sorry, it's a rule of the house, but I could arrange a compromise by serving a dessert with each of your drinks.' This was offered with a sweet smile. My stomach groaned at the thought.

'Can we compromise a bit more and share one dessert?' I asked, starting to get a bit fed up with all this protocol just to get a cup of coffee. The other three nodded and in support of this suggestion, Sally tapped her full stomach, and said, 'were stuffed!' The smile on the sweet face crumbled a little as she turned to leave.

Five minutes later the drinks, a bowl of mixed flavoured ice-cream – the cheapest dessert on the menu – four spoons and the bill were brought on an expensive-looking tray. The sweet smile had disappeared completely. She asked if we'd mind paying the bill straightaway; then clutching her expensive-looking tray, she left us in peace. We never saw her again, even though we lingered in the luxury of that beautiful terrace long after the ice-cream and drinks were consumed. Just as the sun almost touched the horizon, Lil suddenly jumped up saying that we'd better get going.

Four chairs were positioned in a straight line outside our shack. Its four occupants sat stony-faced with arms folded; a stance which didn't alter, even when we waved happily, as Lil drove slowly by.

'What's up with them?' was Sally's hurt remark, at being snubbed.

'Let me do the talking,' said Lil, as she parked alongside George's car, aware that trouble was looming. Unfortunately, her conversational excuses to George were lost in the noise of the bombarding accusations of Alice and Sylvia, along the lines of they were worried and we were selfish.

I thought of the number of mobile phones that could have been easily used, but before I had a chance to contribute to this little drama, George had made a hasty exit, with Lil following close behind.

After such an eventful day, none of us had the energy for anything other than a quiet night in. We added two more chairs to the four that were still outside, and positioned them in a more friendly arrangement. And, by positioning a large, upturned cardboard box in the centre of our friendly arrangement, a perfect surface was made for drinks and snacks. We changed into our pyjamas prior to sitting down, unperturbed by the curious looks from our neighbours. Thankfully, the earlier disharmony dissipated as we all laughed about the funny side of our little escapade and in the moonlit, fragrant warmth of the evening, we enjoyed several hours of companionable chit-chat.

11

Monday 18th April 2005 deserves to be included in the records of Social History, due to a wonderful and very unusual event. Sylvia had risen at 6.30a.m, and actually prepared breakfast for June and Carol.

It was assumed – admittedly by me – that she must have lost at a game of cards and this was her forfeit, instead of a fistful of dollars. But no, I was reliably informed that it was done with a genuine spirit of goodwill. With such an auspicious start and the forecast of another hot, sunny day, we set out with smiles on our faces for Bondi Beach – another one of Lil's 'must do' places on her itinerary.

By mid-morning we'd arrived at the heart of Australia's thriving, surfing paradise. The place was alive with an energy matched only by the huge, rolling waves that crashed incessantly onto the fine, white sand. Keeping well back from the salt spray of the turbulence, a carpet of colourful beach towels were laid out to secure our territory on the beach. Five of the girls dashed off to the waters edge, eager to take part in the watery activity of this famous beach; but only by dipping their feet, then dashing back like small children squealing with delightful fear that the next wave might cover them completely. I sat very contentedly on the towels with Alice, watching and taking in the atmosphere of this natural phenomenon. It was a tremendous thrill to witness at first hand the dozens of surfers slicing through the water; displaying a skill of balance and coordination that was honed to perfection.

Half an hour later the girls returned breathless from exertion and ready to sunbathe. Alice and I were now ready to peruse the beachside shops, and Lil was ready for her morning coffee. The three of us set out, leaving the remainder applying their Factor 6 sun block in temperatures that must have been at least 26C.

For the third time I waited in a queue for the one changing cubicle of the upmarket beachwear store, clutching a bikini. The first two had been discarded, even though I'd been convinced of their suitability when taking them from the rail. Scores of young, sun- kissed women, wearing similar bikinis to the ones I'd just tried, had walked by whilst I was sitting on the towels and they'd looked gorgeous. I was aware that my size 12 figure wasn't bad, but something disconcerting happened to it when I stood before the full length mirror of the changing cubicle. The harsh, artificial lighting emphasised every line and flaw of a body that had danced through more than five decades of music. This left me feeling quite depressed. Alice had found her heart's desire ages ago, and Lil had just entered the store, surprised to find us still here – which only added to my frustration. This time round it was necessary to remove my glasses before pulling the bikini top over my head and not wanting to drop them, I handed them to Lil. All the blemishes miraculously disappeared, along with the detail of my surroundings. As my smiling face peeped through the curtain announcing, 'This is the one,' I heard Alice whisper under her breath, 'Thank God for that.' And I, in turn, thanked God that at least my hearing was in perfect working order.

On reflection, the peace offering had been a bad idea and it was rejected as though it was something I'd just scraped off the bottom of my shoe, instead of the tasty remains of our overlarge lunches. Sally was red in the face with agitation and sunburn as she blurted out, 'We don't want your leftovers, we want to sit down properly and order what *we* want. Where've you been all this time?'

After leaving the beachwear store Alice, Lil and myself had enjoyed checking out the individual clothing shops situated along the bustling, beachfront road. Due to the time of year, reduction sales were commonplace and price tags stamped with 70% off, were the perfect lure for me and Alice to purchase a few more presents for taking home. This hadn't taken too long, and as we returned to the others, arms filled with expensive looking carrier bags containing items costing as little as one dollar, a happy excitement flowed between us all.

The mood was spoilt when I'd mentioned that I was starving and asked if they'd mind waiting until we'd had something to eat before leaving us at base camp with all the bags; once they'd disappeared I knew we wouldn't see them for hours. Grudgingly it was agreed that the three of us could once again shoot off and find somewhere to eat – so long as that was all we did.

Every eating place was busy and the one we'd settled on was the busiest; reasoning that busiest meant best food and prompt service. But it took ages to get served and when the food finally arrived, with a statement from the overly chatty English waitress that the café would soon be closing, we decided to have half the order wrapped as a take-away for the others.

Between the two of us, we carried everything; including the rejected food – which Alice insisted would do for this evening's supper – to a shady, grassed slope overlooking the beach. The effect of the earlier rebuke faded as we relaxed on the towels and reviewed our bargains. Lil had disappeared with the others, probably needing another coffee.

Their moods were much improved by the time they returned with arms full of designer carrier bags and stomachs replete from fish, chips and beer. The afternoon was disappearing fast, leaving just enough time for a few more photographs, before seeking out the bus stop and heading back to Ramsgate.

'We are not staying in again tonight – especially reading a soddin' book – we're on bloody ho-li-day,' screeched Sylvia. I knew before I'd finished voicing the suggestion, that I'd made a terrible faux pas for the second time today. It wasn't just Sylvia firing the verbal refusal, she had a backing group of four – not quite as loud and shockingly to the point as her – but agreeing all the same.

The days seemed to be passing much more quickly now that we'd settled into a familiar routine and naturally, everyone wanted to squeeze in as much pleasure as possible, before they slipped away completely. For me, reading a book at the end of an energetic day happened to be very pleasurable, but I wasn't going to argue the point; especially as I didn't have Lil as an ally. She had gone home to spend the evening with George, no doubt relaxing with a book in front of her, whilst having a lucid conversation with her beloved. A feat I've never been able to master.

Two, sad-looking chaps sitting at the bar were the only other customers in the large room of our local RSL club. Piped music filled the airwaves, but even the upbeat melody of the Beatles singing 'Love me do' didn't make an iota of difference to their demeanour. Their heads turned slightly at the loud scraping noise of the two tables being pushed together, before retreating back to their solemn pool of private thoughts.

'Right, I'll get the first round, give us the purse, Marg,' said Sylvia, eager to get the session rolling. Or maybe she found the two sad faces at the bar a tempting challenge for her engaging attributes.

'I'll have a sparkling mineral water please,' I said, handing her the kitty purse. I happened to feel very thirsty due to the accidental, over-seasoning of the rescued food we'd eaten for supper. I waited for another barrage of abuse, but loud tuts and strange looks were all that followed.

The bottle of water landed unceremoniously before me with a dull thud; there was no accompanying glass, Sylvia picked up her bottle of beer and proceeded to pour it down her throat; keeping her eyes riveted on me. I understood the silent challenge, but I wasn't going to play along, instead I walked back to the bar and asked for a glass.

'You're not like the rest of us, you must be one of the milkman's,' she provoked brazenly, as I proceeded to pour the water into the glass; then stopped suddenly as the effervescent liquid almost boiled over into my lap.

'She's drunk already,' Sylvia chuckled, encouraging my other sisters into her mischief.

My mind was still wrestling with the statement concerning the milkman. I mentally ran through the many positive attributes that I'd come by, via Dad's genetic makeup. I then thought of the unwanted varicose veins that he'd passed on to me, as well as 50% of my siblings. Sylvia mistook my thoughtfulness for sulking, 'I'm only joking, get a proper drink down ya, it'll put a smile on you're face.'

Then she started to sing along to the current song that was being played – either to prove her point, or dispel what she mistakenly thought was a developing bad atmosphere.

Within twenty minutes the two chaps at the bar were bent over in laughter, as Sylvia boomed out one of her hilarious comedy performances; which included a lot of personal details about water tablets and frequent visits to the loo. I was just grateful that the personal details were all hers. As I watched her performing, my mind travelled back to the winter of 1958.

A dangerous strain of Asian flu was sweeping the country; leaving many fatalities in its wake. The whole of our family was affected to some degree, except Mum and me. Sylvia, who was under two- years- old at the time, was left fighting for her young life, in the grip of Double Pneumonia. She was the beautiful baby of the family; her corn silk ringlets framed an angelic face that brought a smile to even the most cheerless of people. It was devastating to visit the hospital and be compelled to view her through a glass window – lying even more confined and concealed in an oxygen tent. Death had become commonplace in the vulnerable during that fated winter, and we knew in our hearts that she could be lost to us forever.

My family – as many people suppose due to our size – are not Catholic, in fact we're not religious at all,(in the accepted sense of the word).

I was ten years old at the time of the Asian flu. My best friend was religious, and a regular visitor to the local Catholic Church. I would join her sometimes, content to wait in the background whilst she fulfilled her duties before being allowed out to play.

During the time of Sylvia's hospitalisation, each member of the family found their own way of dealing with the crisis. I personally became religious for two weeks. I would enthusiastically follow my friend around the church mimicking everything she did and when we knelt to pray my thoughts were on one thing only. I prayed so hard for

*Sylvia's recovery – promising all kinds of good deeds and
changes in my behaviour – if only He would make her well
again. I even lit a candle one day, paying a penny for it
instead of buying sweets.*

My prayers of course were answered. I can't remember
the promises I made to Jesus, or whether I fulfilled any of
them, but I do remember the happiness and joy when Sylvia
finally came back home.

As a consequence of this unfortunate crisis she became
even more precious to us, and her every whim and fancy was
indulged; which created a new phenomenon for our
household – a spoilt child. As she grew and her position as
youngest was superseded by two more babies she found a
new way to gain the attention of her parents and siblings –
making us laugh. She shrugs off the hardest knocks with a
humour that's as infectious as that dreaded Asian flu, but I
know for sure that underneath the hard, carefree exterior, lies
a Sylvia that's as soft as Turkish delight.

'Are you, looking forward to the Blue Mountains trip
Marg?' asked Carol, touching my arm and bringing me back
to the conversation.

'Definitely,' I said with a broad smile. My full attention
kicked in as I remembered we still hadn't sorted out our
lodgings for the last week of our stay and that it was
paramount to get this done in the next two days. Our earlier
plans had been jeopardised when George, along with Alice
and Sally, had driven to view the two, three-bedded rooms of
the tackier motel, to give their opinions on the benefits of
staying there. The result was plenty of opinions but no
benefits. George, when asked said nothing; the derisory scoff
spoke for him. Sally used the word scruffy about eight times

in the two long sentences she used to let us know that we wouldn't be staying there. Alice just said that she thought we could do better than that.

As another tray of drinks arrived, our conversation continued around the forthcoming trip and what was sensible to take to wear. I had visited Lil on my own for a month, five years earlier and the two of us had enjoyed a four-day trip to the mountains, so I wasn't surprised when Sylvia asked *me* if we would need to take walking boots. What had surprised me was the unmistakable look of trepidation in her eyes each time the subject of the mountains came up.

'Well naturally, but we'll need more than walking boots to get around, there are no made up roads and paths. We'll need to get some strong rope and picks before Thursday.' She half smiled at my response, but she couldn't quite conceal her fear, and, to my shame, I decided there and then to take full advantage of this chink in her hard exterior.

12

Although rain had been predicted several times over the last few days we awoke once again to a hot golden sun, surrounded by an uninterrupted, azure blue sky. It was particularly appreciated today, because an enormous pile of laundry needed to be washed and dried. We'd arranged for most of our clothes – packed in the largest suitcases – to be taken to Lil's house for the duration of the mountain trip, so it was imperative to get the task completed by the end of the day.

Alice was already up and from the sound of it, preparing breakfast, even though it wasn't her turn. She was also humming a lively tune, which was even more unusual as silence was her preferred mode for entering a new day (unless one of her younger siblings had been out later than her – then she would enter the role of Second Mother, demanding to know everything).

Intrigued, I climbed out of bed and joined her in the kitchen area.

'Good morning Alice, you obviously slept well,' I said cheerfully, eager to add to this happy atmosphere and find out its cause.

'You sit down, Marg, breakfast is almost ready, Sally's just finishing her shower.' She carried on humming adding a few *la la las* for good measure, but no explanation was forthcoming. I did as I was bid, content in the knowledge that all would be revealed soon, because I could read Sally like a book.

Sally emerged from the shower room, rosy cheeked and smelling as fresh as a highly scented daisy. I studied her face as she sat opposite me at the small table, but could tell instantly that she was as baffled as I was.

The small talk throughout breakfast centred around all the unselfish little tasks that Alice was prepared to do, in order that we – meaning me and Sally – would have plenty of time to carry out the aforementioned laundering. Sally's eyes moved over to her purse, perched in its usual place by the television; I knew what she was thinking. After retrieving it, she half-turned her back to Alice and counted the larger notes secreted in its deepest leather folds. I was also doing some mental arithmetic as to what money I had left to spend freely.

Alice's birthday had fallen two days before we left England, and as this birthday was her sixty-fifth it was also the last day of a job that she'd enjoyed for years and which had provided her with a much needed supplement to her husband's pension. She'd been given no choice in the matter, even though she was happy and more than capable to carry on working.

'Do you need a borra?' Sally blurted out, needing to know what she was up against, because of her own tight budget.

'No, course I don't, I've got plenty of money left,' replied Alice, in a relaxed, carefree manner. A brief glance, with the hint of a shrug, passed between me and Sally. Silence fell as we continued our breakfast.

All the possibilities for her behaviour were systematically covered in my head as I ate my food. She wouldn't want to borrow any of my clothes; they were four sizes too small, my shoes were a size too big, and she had enough cosmetics of her own, to sink a battleship. I studied her face, which seemed to emit an extra healthy glow that I'd failed to notice before today. I'd been too focussed on the changing shades of her earlier bruising. She couldn't have fallen in love; there hadn't been enough privacy between us, for even a sly kiss on the side. I gave up before I gave myself a headache.

94

Alice jumped up to clear the table the second I took my last mouthful of food, making it obvious that she didn't need our help. With her back turned towards us, and the hot tap turned fully on filling the sink, she said hesitantly, 'Marg, you know you were saying the other day how a holiday should be all about doing whatever you wanted to do?'

Before answering, I thought of the denied choice to read my book the evening before and then back to the day of the football match when we were all press-ganged into the blue and white fiasco of ball kicking. But instead of voicing these thoughts, I said, 'Well, its true our personalities differ, but we made this trip together and it's good to spend that time together as much as possible.' This response was more of a reminder to me, than a reply to Alice's statement.

Alice's return to the conversation took a little while. Her body, still viewed from the back, shook with the unnecessary scrubbing of the cereal bowls, creating a rising level of soapy water that began to seep into her pushed up sleeves.

'I've decided to have an hour at Bingo this morning,' she suddenly burst out – reminding me of a frightened teenager having to tell her strict parents that she'd got herself pregnant. She then fired out a whole stream of reasons why she should be allowed to do it. One being she hadn't seen a bingo card for twelve days. She finished her flurry with, 'I'll only be gone for an hour and it's only a ten minute walk, round corner.'

'Don't you mind going on your own?' I enquired to Alice's rear end, wanting to make absolutely clear that I wasn't going to be coerced into spending any of my time in a Bingo hall. Sally was a little nonplussed, but firm in her interruption.

'There's no way I'm going to Bingo, Alice. I don't go at home, so I'm definitely not going while I'm on holiday.'

'Oh, I don't mind going on my own,' said Alice, obviously feeling bold now that she'd unburdened her secret. 'Anyway I think Sylvia and Carol might want to go, just for a change of scenery.'

A mental picture of our local beach; with its soft white sand, clear blue water and salt-laden fresh air compared to a room, crammed with mainly elderly people, heads bent in earnest, whilst an inane voice rolled out number after number and woe betide any poor soul who needed to cough or say they didn't hear the last number called. The hostile looks and shushes given out are enough to make you shrink to the size of a pebble, causing you to miss even more numbers.

'Oh, I'm sure Sylvia will go with you Alice, there's all this washing to get done and she'll want to be well out of the way,' said Sally, a little put out.

'Let them go,' I said, 'It doesn't take six people to load the machines and hang out washing. Besides, they might win the Jackpot then we can all have a room to ourselves for the last week.'

I find one of the most satisfying things in the usually dull world of domestic chores, is standing back to view a line of freshly laundered washing that you've just hung out; especially when it's drying, in a sun-laden breeze. The evocative smell of clothes dried in this natural way is impossible to imitate; no matter how cleverly packaged and marketed the box of chemicals might be. The arduous work of years ago – before washing machines were invented, and women spent almost all day slaving over this back-breaking task – is probably still rooted in my psyche; a reminder of how easy life is today, by comparison.

With my portion of the laundry well and truly over, I decided to join Lil in a trip to Hurstville. She needed to do a few chores of her own in the town and I wanted to change my English pounds into much needed Australian dollars. Sally was packing up her large suitcase – which almost filled the space on the double bed when it was open – so she appreciated having the cabin to herself. June had been left in charge of next door's laundry and the packing, because Sylvia, Carol and Alice had gone to Bingo.

'Three chances to win the Jackpot,' they shouted as we waved them off.

As Lil drove out to Hurstville I performed my usual task of controlling the air con, by turning it on for five minutes then off for ten. We chatted amiably about what each one of us had done that morning. She too had done a large wash, in preparation for our trip. She had also contacted the supervisor of the posh motel and managed to secure two, three-bedded rooms, for the same price as the large, one-bath family room. The unburdening relief, at having this final week's accommodation sorted, proved just how much it had been bothering me. The only thing preventing me from throwing my arms around Lil in gratitude was her nerve-racking driving on the busy Sydney roads. I beamed my brightest smile and promised her an extra large skinny latte as soon as we got parked.

Hurstville Shopping Centre had changed little in the five years since I was last here. Sales were everywhere as before, but this time it was end of summer season bargains, instead of the remains from the winter season. I'd intended to be good and resist the temptation of bargain hunting, but once I had the wherewithal in currency I could spend, two irresistible items found there way into my clutches. I made the excuse that we'd need a few posh clothes for the evening dinners at the mountains motel; convincing Lil to join me, as we went to town on the racks of elegant tops.

The Chinese gift shop was not only crowded with people, dozens of boxes filled with newly arrived stock lay about the floor waiting for the one, overworked assistant to find enough time to empty them. I'd been looking to buy a set of hair ornaments as a small gift for June, who'd taken to borrowing mine and this seemed like the ideal place to find them.

I found what I wanted within two minutes, but knew it would take five times that long to pay; looking at the length of the queue. I inched slowly forward, sweeping my eyes along the shelves of inexpensive knick-knacks, wondering why on earth anyone would want to buy them. Lil, unable to keep still for long, wandered around the store.

Almost at the pay counter, I noticed a box of whistles, reminding me of my schooldays, and in particular, standing to attention at the sound of a sharp, piercing trill. I picked one up and without thinking gave a sharp blow. All these years later and the effect was still the same. All but one of the shops occupants stopped dead in their tracks. The odd one fell back in fright, tripping backwards over a badly placed box of stock and knocking down a newly built pyramid of boxed kangaroos.

Lil grabbed one of the whistles, saying that it was just what she needed for the mountains. Well if she was going to play teacher, I wanted to be able to respond in kind, so I took one, making sure the suspension cord was a different colour to hers. The worried-looking assistant served us straight away and almost escorted us off the premises.

The showers forecast for the late afternoon didn't materialise. Sad news for the Australians who needed the rain desperately for gardens already parched from a restrictive watering ban, but definitely good news for us. As

Lil left for home I handed her the neatly folded sheets and towels that she'd loaned us and carried indoors the remaining pile of sweetly-smelling, completely dried laundry. June had hung her long line of washing out much later in the day, when the sun had moved off the area and as a consequence, her washing wasn't dry enough to bring in.

'Congratulations, I heard you won at Bingo,' I said happily, handing Alice a celebratory mug of tea. She returned my smile with an even broader one and a look of pride that added at least two inches to her height.

'I woke up feeling really lucky; that's why I wanted to go,' she informed, but was still as coy as the others, as to how much of a fortune she'd actually won. We didn't need an upgrade to a better motel now that Lil had worked her magic, but a champagne dinner to celebrate our last day in the shacks would be very nice.

'I didn't win a fortune,' Alice continued, losing the two inches of height and changing my fantasy of champagne dinner to a fish and chip supper. 'I won a twenty dollar gift voucher to spend at the supermarket. I'll change it for three films to take to the mountains.'

The beautiful, classical guitar music, heard via my small digital radio, added to the tranquil mood I'd created in the cabin. It was only eight-fifteen but I was already in my pyjamas, supported by a mound of pillows on the large bed, reading my book in the soft glow of the bedside lamp. Not a single voice had contradicted my choice of how I'd wanted to spend this evening – when my five sisters had again decided to visit the local club for a drink.

A soft tapping on the cabin door brought me out of my reverie and the current scenario that I was reading about. I opened the door to find Lil standing there, looking confused at finding me in my nightwear.

'I've been sent to come and get you,' she said, blaming the others for the intrusion, as she picked up on the ambience of the cabin.

'I thought you were done here for the day,' I said, avoiding her statement and trying to keep disappointment out of my voice.

'Well, George said, make the most of this time together, you're already halfway through the three weeks, so here I am.'

Five minutes later with arms linked, we walked down the dark road leading to the club, where the others waited for all seven of us to be together. About halfway down the dark road Lil noticed a partially concealed gap, which she thought might be a short cut to the club. The clouds had thickened even more around the moon, blocking out any helpful light to indicate if this was a good idea or not. I'd witnessed Lil going down several blind alleys in her car, so I was a little more circumspect. But as her eyes are sharper than mine I decided to give her the benefit of the doubt; clinging on to her arm even tighter, because without my glasses – which were in my bag – I'm almost as blind as a bat.

Fifty yards or so into the narrow ally we froze. A large dog's head suddenly appeared over a side gate, accompanied by a menacing snarl that soon developed into wild barking. We turned tail and shot back to the road in double quick time, frightened but giggling. As we entered the club, still hyped up from our narrow escape of being eaten alive, all heads turned in our direction; well, all five heads of my sisters, because apart from them the place was deserted.

Empty or not it didn't spoil the couple of wonderful hours spent chatting, or *camping*, which is the correct Lancashire way of describing a good-hearted conversation. Sylvia had us in stitches yet again, as she continued the saga of her frequent visits to the loo, trying to convince us that her overweight body was due to a surplus of fluid.

'This is what all this is,' she announced, grabbing hold of two handfuls of her enormous waistline.

'You mean its liquid fat,' someone said amongst peels of laughter.

'No, it's just liquid and the tablets will sort it,' she replied emphatically.

'Wouldn't it be easier to just drink less in the first place?' I came in, genuinely concerned.

'No, my doctor said I've got to drink plenty,' she continued, convinced of her facts.

'She meant water or fruit juice,' I said exasperated.

'My doctor's a **he** not a **she**,' concluded Sylvia and quickly changed the subject.

The purchase of the two whistles came into the conversation, prompting a few niggled responses of why we couldn't all have one. Lil explained, as if to a class of eight year olds, that it would be too confusing having seven whistles going off at random, and besides, she continued, they were bought solely as a means of communication in an emergency. Sylvia, concerned at the content of the last few words, but bold from a belly full of liquid beer, said with a sneer,

'Why would any one need to use a whistle?'

Jumping straight into the gap that was left for a reply I couldn't resist continuing the wind up.

'Sylvia, if you're halfway up a mountain and a dense mist develops – and it's not unusual for this to happen – the whistles will be our only way of communicating where we are. Oh! and that reminds me Lil, we still need to get rope and picks.' Sylvia's chair made a loud grating noise as she shot off to the loo, for the umpteenth time.

13

A distinct noise dragged me from sleep and transported me back to my home in the lush countryside of Devon. It was pouring with rain. Opening my eyes and allowing several seconds of confusion to pass, I was brought back to the reality of the shack and a feeling that I hadn't been in bed very long. I was right; the cooker clock showed fourteen minutes past midnight.

A smug relief washed over me as I thought of heavy laundry, dried and put away. Then as the downpour developed into a deluge, I remembered with dismay that the washing from next door was still left hanging in the drenching, watery night. Instinct kicked in and I was already sitting up with one leg out of bed – alert and ready to run outside to retrieve the items – before common sense pushed me back onto my pillow and into a mental state of sombre acceptance. No doubt by now the sodden items would have been dragged down to the level of the softened, sparsely grassed area, where a combination of grass green and mud brown will be mingling with the other colours of the beach towels.

As we'd walked back from the club just a couple of hours ago, we'd sensed rain in the air and even felt a few spit spots. I'd reminded June about the washing and offered to help bring it inside. Her understandable response had been to leave it on the line as it wasn't quite dry and there was no where suitable in the shack to air it off. In retrospect, putting the whole load in the dryer before going out would have been the best plan.

Another watery sound brought me to the surface of consciousness once again. It was Sally flushing the loo, which automatically brought on the need for me to do the same. Four thirty-five was now showing on the clock and the rain was still hammering down – adding to the noise of the filling toilet system.

'Next door's washing will be draped in mud,' I said to Sally in a hushed voice, as I passed the bunk that she was struggling to get back into.

'Serves them right, they should have got on with it earlier in the day like we did, instead of messing around and thinking of bingo.'

I climbed back into bed with the vain hope of securing a couple more hours of sleep amid the symphonic sounds of heavy rain, Alice's snoring and a few isolated parrot squawks.

Alice was up first again, making encouraging sounds with the kettle, teapot and cups. The rain had now eased to a steady drizzle.

'Did you hear that downpour in the night?' I asked her, wrapping the rarely-used dressing gown around me to help stave off the unusual damp chill in the air.

'No I was asleep.'

'Well it's our last day in the shacks, Alice, what a pity it has to be a damp and miserable one, after all that lovely sunshine.'

'As it's our last day Sylvia and Carol are going to join me for another hour at bingo.'

There wasn't the slightest hint of flexibility, or any sign of yesterday's deliberation, as she imparted this obviously, pre-arranged news.

With breakfast over and cleared away, the hive of activity that developed in each shack – after a boardroom style consultation – was to be much admired. June was given sole responsibility over the rescuing and making good of the fated laundry. Carol and Sylvia were packing their large suitcases ready for Lil to transport to her house. This had to be done by 10-45a.m in order to grab that precious hour at bingo; so they were moving at a speed that would have impressed anyone, including Lil. In our shack, the three of us just kept out of each others way as much as possible, whilst packing and sorting what was needed for the mountains.

A pile of unwanted items was steadily growing in the far corner nearest the front door, conveniently placed for taking to the rubbish bins. Alice hovered over the pile – an inflated football trophy tucked under each arm – unable, even now, to relinquish the bloody things. I approached her brandishing a large safety pin, 'Let me solve the problem once and for all.'

'No, I'll give 'em to the children,' she said, disappearing out of the door.

Twenty minutes later she was back, still holding the plastic monstrosities and wearing a hurt look on her face.

'You can't even give them away, not even to small, unsuspecting children,' I jeered. She threw one at me, then quickly grabbed it back, knowing there was a safety pin lurking nearby.

'Tell you what,' I said, in a more conciliatory voice, 'Let's go for a walk and dispose of them ritualistically.'

'You mean like, letting 'em float out to sea, so a far off ship can find 'em and wonder who won 'em?'

'No, the oceans are polluted enough,' I cut in, thinking more along the line of dumping them in the nearest dustbin, but saying, 'We'll think of something fitting.'

'Stop messing about you two,' shouted Sally, getting frustrated with the piles of clothes that resisted her every attempt to fit them into her large suitcase. 'I'm never, ever, taking this much stuff away with me again. I know we're going into Hurstville this afternoon, but I'm not buying a thing, in fact, I'll be leaving a lot of this stuff behind when we leave Australia.' She glared at Alice, who was still clutching the inflated cups in her arms.

'Chuck 'em out Alice, we haven't got room for any...'

Alice was out of the door before the last word assaulted her ears. The ritual I had in mind, was photographing her throwing the offending items into the tour park recycling bin. She complied meekly with a slight, tight smile and I have the photograph to prove it.

There was the sweet, clean smell of freshly watered grass as I slowly walked back to the shack. The rain had finally stopped and a shy sun peeped out from the edge of a breakaway cloud. Alice had gone on ahead, unburdened; she could now concentrate on her chores, before heading off to bingo.

As I approached our shack, Sylvia's voice could be heard, loud and clear. She was remonstrating – her index finger prodding the air – just a few inches from June's face.

'Don't you ever interrupt my conversation again, it's my bloody phone, I'm paying for the soddin' call and it's got nothing to do with you how long I soddin' well talk on it.'

I felt for June, especially as this verbal lashing was taking place out in the open where the occasional passer by felt the need to give this domestic scene a wide birth. But she stood her ground with hands on hips, allowing Sylvia to run out of steam.

These two had been naturally very close since they were toddlers; there were just two years between them, so this outburst, although not commonplace, was manageable for June. After all she'd produced three sons in the space of five years, so fights and tantrums must have been dealt with on a daily basis.

'Your frightening the parrots, what's going on?' I aimed at Sylvia, trying to lighten the situation, as June turned tail and headed for the laundry room.

'I'm trying to 'av a conversation with Paul. I'm concerned about *mi* daughter-in-law and I don't need her (she aimed a finger at June's retreating back) giving me that (she moved her fingers to imitate a pecking beak) in my other ear.'

'How is Fiona, surely the baby must be due by now?'

'If nothing 'appens today, they're 'aving her in tomorrow to induce the birth.'

'I know you must be worried, Sylvia, but I'm sure everything will be fine.' She gave a heavy sigh and stepped back into her shack, leaving a void of silence behind that only lasted a few seconds before the squawking parrots reclaimed their birthright.

The laundry room was empty except for June, who, on hearing my footsteps, began frantically waving her hands in the air, to clear it of cigarette smoke.

'It's only me,' I called, knowing full well that this hand waving was a regular exercise of hers since we'd been staying here. A rigid 'No Smoking' policy operated throughout the park; unless of course you were out in the open air. Under normal circumstances, June, being the only smoker amongst us – except for Carol who succumbs to the odd one – keeps the habit confined to a social activity whilst having a beer. But no doubt, there have been several stressful situations that have caused her to reach for the ciggies and disregard the safety rules. Only yesterday, Carol confessed, in fits of laughter, how she and June had been having a crafty smoke in their shack, when they heard Lil about to enter. The two of them – with hands wafting the air – retreated into the bathroom area and hid in the shower cubicle, where they had remained – a towel stuffed in their mouths to stifle their nervous laughter – until Lil had left.

'Do you need any help?' I asked June, hoping to find out what caused the mini eruption.

'No thanks, Marg, I didn't need to rewash anything, I'm just spinning, then tumble drying them.'

'What was all that about with Sylvia?' I asked, anxious to quell any growing resentment. But my fears proved to be unfounded when she replied, without any rancour, that she was only trying to stop Sylvia going off at a tangent on the phone, when the calls cost a fortune and there wasn't the time, if she wanted to have that hour at bingo. 'Don't worry about it Marg, she's uptight and worried about Fiona and the baby.'

At five minutes to mid-day I stood outside the RSL club accompanied by Sally and June, waiting for our bingo-addicted sisters to emerge amongst the throng of mainly elderly ladies. You could tell at a glance the folks that had been touched by Lady Luck and this easy guessing game kept the three of us happily entertained whilst we waited.

Ten minutes later, as we'd almost given up hope of seeing them, our three sauntered into view. Carol had the broadest smile and a jaunty step. 'I won twice,' she said happily, 'A full house and a Dolly Parton.' A mental image of a life-size, blow up doll – sporting extra large breasts – came to mind and as I tried to connect this to the age and gender of the folks I'd just observed, Carol interrupted my thoughts. 'A Dolly Parton is three numbers on the top line, two in the middle and one at the bottom – I've got twenty five dollars to spend at the supermarket.'

108

'What about you two?' I said expectantly, 'You were so long in coming out we thought you must be waiting for several winning tokens.'

'What we were waiting for,' said Sylvia, in a slow, deliberate, loud voice, 'Was to have a pee! These oldies can't 'arf move quick at the end of a session to get to the toilets first.'

The shack looked far more spacious and even *deluxe*, now that the bulk of our possessions had been transported to Lil's, and as I surveyed the space that had been our home for the last ten days, I was filled with pangs of sentimentality. I'd said my 'goodnight, God bless to Sally', as she'd climbed into her bunk for the last time, done with an agile skill that will probably never be called upon again. Alice was alongside me in the big bed, and seeing me reach for my book she sorting out a magazine to read.

Within five minutes a loud vibrating snore told me that she was asleep, even though she was sitting bolt upright with her glasses on, and the magazine positioned quite correctly in front of her face. I nudged her gently, 'Alice, take your glasses off and lay down.'

'I can't see to read, without them,' she said in a thick voice. One minute later the snoring came again. This time I took her glasses off, removed the magazine and turned out the light. All she did was slip down onto her pillow, snuggle down under the sheet and continue to snore. I felt envious of the ease in which she had slipped into sleep, leaving me very much still grounded in the current day.

The bus had taken all of us into Hurstville for the afternoon – after being seduced by yesterday's account of the many bargains to be had in its bustling shopping centre. We all came away with bags of clothes or accessories that were too irresistible for our weak resolve, even though we knew in our hearts they weren't really needed, nor did we have the space in our cases to carry them. But what fun it had been procuring them. We tried on and admired, compared and discussed literally dozens of items between us, always checking the labels for the keenest priced items – to help salve our consciences. Sally, true to her word, and now the proud owner of a tried and tested life lesson, didn't buy any items of clothing or adornment. She did have a carrier bag of something, but we'll give her the benefit of the doubt and say it was developed photographs and edibles.

The face of the bright moon hung centrally in the window alongside my side of the bed illuminating everything in the shack. Both Alice and Sally were quietly sleeping, so in all honesty, I couldn't use them as an excuse for my wakefulness. I was excited about our imminent trip to the mountains, and I felt sure that this, coupled with the effect of the almost dazzling moonshine, was preventing me from falling asleep.

I turned away from the window, closed my eyes, and pictured in turn all the people that I loved; a mental exercise that always brought on a feeling of wellbeing and relaxation.

On the other side of the globe, on the small island of Lanzarote, Barry, I hoped would be relaxing and enjoying himself. We've enjoyed many winter holidays there and even toyed with the idea of buying a small apartment. But lately, Barry's dislike of the English climate has spread to include all things English; from the current Government, down to the price of petrol. In short, he wants to become one of the many thousands who are deserting their homeland for sunnier climes and a more affordable-standard of living.

Remnants of the earlier sentimental pangs – connected with leaving the shack – blossomed into a full-blown panic attack at the thought of selfishly deserting my children and granddaughter, in order to enjoy a warmer climate. An inner voice warned, 'Don't go there, if you want to get any sleep tonight.' I carefully eased myself out of bed, and using only the light of the silvery moon I warmed myself a cup of milk – hoping with all my heart that this would help take me to where I wanted to be.

14

In spite of the reduced amount of sleep, I rose early enough to keep pace with the rest of the gang; to vacate the shacks at the expected time of 10.00 a.m. By 9.30 a.m, our shack was completely devoid of any sign that three sisters had shared a tiny piece of their lives within its space.

My final chore was to take the used linen to the cabin-maid's laundry area, including the extra bedding they'd kindly let us use (free of charge), after Lil had taken hers back. This done, I wandered slowly around the tour park, saying a silent goodbye – bringing on the sentimental pangs once again.

On popping my head around next doors cabin – expecting to find it as neat as ours – I was assaulted by a thrown pillow and a shoe. Sylvia was almost lost amongst the billowing sheets of the double bed and Carol and June were beneath it, throwing things in the direction of the door – where I happened to be standing.

'What's going on?' I enquired, taking a long look at my watch, so as to indicate my concern. Sylvia's muffled voice explained in fits and starts, as she dipped in and out of the clouds of linen, that she'd lost her gold earrings. These earrings apparently held special sentimental value and she was almost certain that she'd taken them out a couple of evenings back, and slipped them under her pillow; hence the near demolition of the bed. Fortunately, all their personal stuff was packed, so I left them to it and returned to the organised calm of our place, where Sally had just made a final cup of tea.

Unfortunately, the thorough strip and search didn't produce the missing earrings. All that could be done was to leave Lil's telephone number at reception, in the unlikely event that they were found.

Lil had secured a three-week holiday break, to be able to spend as much time with us as possible. Whereas George, unfortunately, (although my guess is, he would be thinking, very fortunate) needed to carry on working. This meant that only one vehicle was available for the mountain trip.

Carol and Alice were travelling to the mountains in Lil's car, along with the bulk of the luggage. The remaining four of us were travelling by train, each carrying our own backpack. Before leaving, Lil had given me all the appropriate timetables; covering buses to Hurstville, trains to Sydney Central and trains to Wentworth Falls – our motel destination. The car travellers were expecting to arrive by lunchtime (depending on traffic), but Lil made a point of saying that *we,* would probably arrive before her.

June, Sylvia and Sally chatted amiably on the bus ride to Hurstville, whilst I scanned the timetables – underlining the appropriate train times that would get us to the motel before lunchtime.

We reached Sydney Central in good time, allowing us the opportunity to buy refreshments for eating on the train later. The first meal provided by the motel was the evening meal at 7.00 p.m. and – considering the full-on activity that today was bound to unleash – we all knew, that buying food as an interim, was going to be necessary. What I hadn't taken into consideration, whilst planning the connections, was any time delay in getting from one side of Sydney Central Station to the other.

Each clutching an armful of food and drink, we marched down the walkways of the Rail Network following the signs and directions given by its attendants. It was a long march and twice we were sent the wrong way, fuelling a rising

113

irritation that developed into panic, when we reached our platform with one minute to spare before our train left.

On the opposite side of the platform another train stood idling, waiting only for the platform guard to blow his whistle and allow it to shunt away. I ran up to this guard and asked which train was going to Wentworth Falls, knowing before he answered that I wouldn't quite believe him, because paranoia had now taken the place of panic. He pointed to the other train, then watched open-mouthed as I dashed to a nearby attendant to ask him the same question. His bellowing voice from behind halted everyone on the crowded platform, as he articulated in slow motion the train's number and where it was going. He then walked over to the train until his outstretched, pointing finger made contact with its heavy steel door and continued – in an even louder voice – to tell his captive audience that this was definitely the train that madam wanted.

Disappearing into the bowels of the train and locating seating for four, in an area that offered a modicum of privacy, was done without anyone speaking a word. However, as soon as we claimed our territorial space and the train began to move slowly out of the station, our speech returned.

'What's his problem?' asked Sally, speaking to her pre-packed rice pudding as she examined it for spillage onto her sandwiches.

'Doesn't like women!' offered June.

'You mean, they don't like him,' added Sylvia. 'I bet he hasn't had his leg over in months, miserable sod.' Then she began eating what was supposed to be her lunch. I didn't comment, but contributed by boldly sticking out my tongue at the guard, hoping to break his continued stare. It didn't work. So we glared at each other – him from the platform and me from the window seat – until the widening distance between us brought this impasse to an end.

Within five minutes of leaving Sydney we were all tucking into our lunches; not caring that it was still only late morning. As we ate we watched the passing scenery change; from bustling city to suburban sprawl and on to a blend of soft natural countryside, interspersed with the odd tin-roofed homestead. By the time we'd finished eating, the train was starting to climb at a steady pace into magnificent views of jagged rocks and deep crevasses.

Five years ago when I'd visited the mountains, Lil and I had travelled by car, which was pleasant enough, but this was something else. The train seemed to cut through the very heart and bones of the lower mountains. Conversation was hushed as we watched in awe the unfolding splendour of this majestic terrain. This was a complete contrast to what we'd experienced in the last ten days, and all too soon we arrived at the simple country station of Wentworth Falls.

The oscillating roar of the traffic made conversation impossible, so we walked in silence and single file down the narrow path than ran alongside the highway.

The vain hope of walking out of the station and jumping straight into a taxi, was dashed within minutes of casting our eyes around the sleepy (not much bigger than a village), mountain town. I'd crossed the road to enquire at an estate agent's office for directions to the motel, leaving the others standing outside the station; just in case a taxi should miraculously drive by. As I'd suspected the motel wasn't far, but, it was positioned on the opposite side of the highway, which involved an ear splitting walk and a tricky crossing up ahead. I relayed all this information to my sisters, who relayed back their preference for riding, not walking.

A middle-aged man was stopped and asked where we might find a taxi. His face had broadened into a smile as he told us there were only two cabs in Wentworth Falls, and he happened to drive one of them.

'Well, what a fortunate coincidence,' I beamed, 'Could you take us to our motel?' His smile didn't alter as he shook his head and said that he was off duty, but he would phone the office and have a word with his pal. I expected him to take out a mobile phone, but no, he carried on walking, God knows where to.

'Where shall we wait and how long do you think he'll be?' I shouted after him. He half turned towards us, the broad smile now looking more like a jeer.

'I can't say how long he'll be, might not come at all, you'll just have to wait and see.'

'I'm walking, you can wait here if you like,' I said, in no mood for any more male chauvinism. June said she didn't mind walking. Sally shrugged her shoulders and said 'whatever,' leaving Sylvia under no illusion as to how we were getting to the motel.

After walking for about a mile the path forked and we were tempted onto the right hand split, which led further inland and away from the assault on our eardrums. But within ten minutes of making this detour, the sound of a ferocious, barking dog, sent us running back to the preferred noise of the traffic. As luck would have it, there, on the opposite side of the highway, was the almost concealed slip road – leading to our sanctuary. Holding on to each other, we prayed and cursed and did whatever each individual needs to do at moments like this, when you literally take your life into your hands. Safely across to the opposite side of those thunderous lanes of speeding vehicles we were filled with a cocktail of emotions – fear, relief and joy.

116

Lil and co. had arrived before us, but I was passed caring about that, the rooms were not quite ready, so no one could accuse us of being late. I wouldn't have missed the scenic train ride for the world, and the other unpleasant events of the journey didn't come anywhere near to cancelling it out.

The communal lounge of the motel was very welcoming; with its large, comfortable sofas and generous provision of tea, coffee and biscuits. Lil added to this, by producing nuts and other light snacks from her car. The only edible item we could contribute was a large bag of black liquorice that I'd bought in Hurstville the day before; but apart from the odd adventurous finger, dipping in to try a small piece, the bag remained almost full.

'I've checked out the situation of the rooms,' announced Lil, going on to explain that ours (meaning hers and mine), was on the ground floor at the back of the motel and had no balcony. Sylvia, June and Carol were to share a three-bedded room on the top floor with a balcony overlooking the front. Alice and Sally's room was on the ground floor, again with a balcony to the front. Lil's words brought beaming smiles to all faces bar mine. I felt a bit miffed that our room was missing the obvious delight of a private, outdoor space; then the thought of the busy highway, passing by the front elevation of the motel, soon quelled the niggardly feelings. There were no balconies at the rear, but there was peace and tranquillity and as Lil had stayed in far more motels than me, I bowed to her superior judgement and common sense to have taken these finer points into consideration.

It was indeed a very quiet and comfortable twin-bedded room and within ten minutes Lil and I were unpacked and heading outside for a gentle stroll in the fresh mountain air.

117

With the highway at our backs, we walked along a leafy country road enjoying the sight and sounds of the many tropical birds. As we were watching the antics of a cheeky Kookaburra – one of Lil's favourite birds – another barking dog spoilt the tranquillity of the moment and sent us hotfooting back to base. I was beginning to wonder at the ratio of dogs to people in this sparsely populated mountain region.

'This room is for the old or disabled,' grumbled Sally, as she pointed out the seat in the shower and the extra wide doorframes.

'Well you are old,' I said playfully, 'and even Alice would find it hard to injure herself in this room.' She gave me a stony look and continued to hang her clothes in the more than ample wardrobe.

Lil and I took the stairs to see how the other three were faring. Sylvia had laid claim to the largest of the three beds that was alongside the farthest wall from the balcony. Carol was sitting next to this on a standard single bed. June had opted, had actually chosen, the smallest facility for sleeping. A put-you-up couch, converted into its present state – a very small single bed. Even worse, its proximity to the balcony doors meant that June would be frantically searching for her complimentary earplugs, before the night was through. I kept my mouth shut, not wanting to spoil the happy atmosphere of the room.

'I hear congratulations are in order?' I said to Sylvia, as I wrapped my arms around her.

'She was born a couple of hours ago and her name is Rea', she said with obvious relief.

We all welcomed Rea into this wonderful world with a toast of bubbly as we sat down to our first evening meal at the motel, dressed fittingly in posh clothes.

An hour or so later we were back in the communal lounge, feeling more than a little tipsy, but well and truly at home in the large comfy sofas. There was no entertainment in the motel on a Thursday evening at this, 'out of season' time of year, so we were in the throes of entertaining ourselves, before disappearing into our respective rooms. We had all agreed that an earlier than usual nights sleep would set us up nicely for the energetic day ahead.

'Charades, but its not Christmas,' wailed a couple of mutinous voices, at Lil's suggestion. Undeterred, she went on to say that Australians play this game all the year round.

'That's because they're arse about face with everything here; I even saw Christmas decorations in the shops! Christ we're still in April.' This was Sylvia, putting in her four-penneth. Lil stood her ground. I've seen Lil galvanise a roomful of total strangers into antics that beggar belief, so *we* were chicken feed in comparison. Besides, she was good at charades and was in the mood for proving it.

There were more than a few surprises, as awkwardness gave way to confidence, aided by the alcohol that still trickled through from the bar next door. Certain members of our sisterhood were clearly good mind readers; picking up the thoughts of the one giving the silent clues within seconds of their arms taking flight.

It was good fun, and I stand witness that every single one of us enjoyed it. But this frivolity, on top of everything else that the day had thrown at us, took its toll and before too long we started to sag. Lil ran through her planned schedule for the following morning, hoping there were enough wide awake brain cells in us to retain it.

Before turning in I tried again to reach Barry via my ancient mobile phone, but neither phoning nor texting could connect us, so I communicated by using a newly purchased postcard from reception, saddened that it would be at least a week before he could read my heartfelt words.

15

Breakfast was a completely different ball game now that we were in an all-inclusive, already-paid for, motel. We could eat as much as we wanted, of whatever was on offer. In fact, we felt obliged to do so; reasoning that a large intake of nourishment in the morning would carry us through until the all-inclusive evening meal, without having to dip into the hard-pressed kitty purse. Gone were all thoughts of calorie counting or health implications. Our plates were filled with such an assortment of food – the standard, full English breakfast seemed puny in comparison.

We emerged from the dining room at a much slower pace than we'd entered and headed straight for our respective bathrooms. According to Lil's schedule we had ten minutes before meeting at reception for the pre-arranged lift to the Blue Mountains Tour Bus. 'All present and correct?' she asked, whistle clearly visible around her neck, reminding me of a particularly bossy teacher who taught us netball and hockey at school.

'Where's your whistle?' she aimed at me, anxious that I hadn't left behind the means to respond to her, if distance was forced upon us. I tapped the bulge hidden beneath my shirt, relieved at last to point out to everyone that I wasn't growing a third breast, but still not bold enough to wear it on the outside, for fear of being tarred with the same officious brush as Lil.

'When we get outside I'll give a good blow so that we know how it sounds,' continued Lil tapping the acoustic pendant – its cord, perfectly colour-keyed to her shirt.

'I think we all know what a bloody whistle sounds like,' cut in Sylvia. She was clearly unnerved now that the mountaineering was imminent, and miffed at Lil, for running

121

through this malarkey, without any regard for her fears and phobias.

'Anyone for liquorice?' I asked, handing round my stash. One or two declined with a slow shake of the head, their thoughts easy to read. Personally, I find liquorice very settling on the stomach, especially after a heavy meal. However, it was drummed into us as kids never to buy liquorice (we, as Lancastrians, knew it as *spanish* in those far off days), because it gave you *the runs*.

The early morning sunshine felt warm on my back as we stood at the end of the slip road, waiting for our all-inclusive lift. It was over seventy degrees and predicted to rise much higher by midday, nevertheless our mode of dress was completely different to the previous ten days. There was no sign of the usual light sandals and skimpy shorts or skirts, worn with low-cut sun tops. Gone too, were all signs of jewellery and make up. Wedding rings and watches were all that remained as adornment, with lip salve taking the place of colourful, glossy lipsticks. Sensible shoes or walking boots with socks, linked perfectly with the long shorts or cut-off trousers, made from strong, cotton material in either beige or grey; tucked into these, were similar coloured shirts. A jumper or jacket – tied around the waist – completed the ensemble. This was to be our day-time uniform for the next three days. The only other items taken were a bottle of water each, purses, sunglasses and cameras; all easily stowed away in our back packs, keeping both hands free to deal with any eventuality.

The minibus dropped us at the small mountain town of Katoomba – which means (if your not familiar with the Aboriginal language) sparkling waters. This was the first of twenty- seven stops that the tour bus was scheduled to take.

Stop number twelve, Echo Point is where we were heading today.

The broad Australian twang of the drivers voice accompanied us through the beautiful scenic landscape, as he proudly pointed out the many features on route – each furnished with a brief potted history. The comparison to our situation on the red tour bus in Sydney (which seemed an age away), surfaced once or twice, reminding me that no matter how much you plan and smooth the way, Sod the law giver, is always waiting in the wings to foul things up.

Looking around at the relaxed, smiling faces of my sisters, happily venturing out on this shared new adventure, I felt certain that nothing could possibly spoil the day. True enough, Sylvia was a bit uptight at what lay ahead, but that was only due to my teasing. She'd soon discover the truth for herself, dispelling the slight hold I'd had on her emotions over the last few days. With the temperature climbing and a blue sky devoid of clouds, mist whether rising or falling – would be non-existent today. I slipped the cord-strung whistle over my head and tucked it into my rucksack, convinced I wouldn't need it.

Twenty-five minutes later we were standing at the famous Echo Point, looking across the broad expanse of the deep wooded valley below. In the distance the tall, rocky ridge was shrouded in a blue haze, showing clearly how the mountains got there colourful name. The foreground was dominated by a triple stand of tall rocks; three jagged fingers pointing towards the clear blue sky. The finger tips were in bright sunshine, the lower mass in shadow, its dark shape spread across the bright green of the valley floor. This finger-like rock formation is known as The Three Sisters, christened by an Aboriginal legend of three beautiful ladies who were turned to stone by their witch doctor father.

Many years ago Mum and Dad had stood at this same vantage point, in awe of its majesty and charmed by its legend. Their descent to the valley below had been by the Scenic Railway, reported to be the steepest in the world. I remember Dad boasting that it went down so fast that it nearly ripped your face off. He had always been very nervous of speed, so at the time, I took this rash statement with a pinch of salt.

Five years ago, I also stood here looking up at a leaden sky, pregnant with threatening rain clouds. The wooded valley was hidden beneath a thick, swirling mist, making it both dangerous and pointless to venture into. I'd felt disappointed and cheated.

Two years prior to my first visit, during the height of Australian summer, my son and his new bride had also enjoyed visiting this place. They'd told me of their descent on foot, into the cool shady realm of the valley, a welcome escape from the searing heat and a chance to see the plants and creatures that are indigenous to this part of the world. I'd seen their photographs of the mountain springs that spilled into rocky basins – for quenching the thirst of those determined enough to find their hiding places.

I feel that determination today. The weather is perfect; I will not be denied.

A slight shove, snapped me out of my preoccupation, as I was herded closer to my sisters and ordered to smile. A passer by had been accosted, with a camera thrust into her hand to record the start of this memorable occasion. Six more cameras were produced, and the same passer by good naturedly performed the role of free photographer to our large sisterhood. Murmurings of needing the loo spread through our group, dispelling the magic of my lofty intentions even more.

As I left the toilet block, I saw Lil a few yards down the first path. She stood with her feet apart, hands on her hips and the whistle positioned in her mouth – reminding me again of the bossy hockey teacher. I would love to have captured the stance on camera, but I could see she was impatient to get going, and the staggered way we were exiting the crowded toilets was testing her enough.

There are many paths leading down to the valley, ranging from very gentle to downright arduous. This, obviously, is to allow for all ages and all physical abilities. The gentle paths are fine if you have all day to spare, or you don't mind doing a partial descent. We wanted to get all the way down, as soon as possible, although we all had our different reasons for doing so.

A sharp blow on the whistle brought everyone's attention into focus, including several dozen tourists (mainly Japanese) who promptly stood to attention. Lil's usual rosy cheeks deepened a shade or two, either with embarrassment or an increased sense of power.

'We're about to reach the 'Devil's Stairway', so let's get in line. I'll go first, and Marg you stay at the back as you've got the other whistle.' Sylvia looked like she was about to dart back into the toilet block, so I took her arm, positioned her in front of me and explained that they were only steps for walking down, climbing with ropes was just a bit of teasing. She didn't look convinced and moved her position to the one in front, putting Sally between us. Silence descended as we walked in single file down the gentle slope of the well-worn preliminary path.

The limestone steps of the 'Devil's Stairway' are chiselled out of the steep rock face, and because of their relative softness, large sections had worn away overtime and had been replaced with robust, steel, open mesh steps. A protecting run of side panels – also constructed in similar open mesh steel – was positioned to waist height, with smooth hand rails running along its top. The whole structure was designed for maximum protection, with minimum interference and obstruction to the breathtaking views, which included the sheer drop beneath our feet.

The silence between us began to break up. It started with a lone, 'bloody 'ell,' muttered softly beneath someone's breath. Then 'Jesus Christ' was blasted out much more forcefully, opening the floodgates for all the profanities known to man. A fear rippled down the line which didn't start at the front. Lil had done this descent several times and as she skipped down the steps, I think she was hoping to spread her confidence down the line. I held no fears, for me the experience was exhilarating. Of my five sisters in between I'd say at least three were not enjoying this descent and at least one was terrified. Several times I called out, 'don't look down,' but the instinctive compulsion to watch your feet, as you manoeuvre a steep, winding, narrow stairway, is understandable.

Approximately one hundred steps down, we reached the first resting post – a shallow, open rock cave, furnished with a couple of benches to give rest to the weary before venturing on downward. Sylvia and Alice made it quite clear that they wouldn't be venturing anywhere, as they sat down on one of the benches and clung to it, like a pair of leeches.

'You go on down, we'll wait here with all the bags,' offered Alice, in a tone of voice that made it clear this was non-negotiable. Everyone except me started to unload their backpacks and hand them over to the clinging pair. I challenged the wisdom of this, pointing out that water, camera, jacket, etc. were all items that could be needed and were no real problem to carry.

'I'm not leaving my bag,' I responded to the strange looks from all my sisters, who flaunted their complete freedom of baggage by stretching their arms in the air, then letting them fall in a mock attempt to touch their toes. What I did hand over to Alice – at Lil's insistence – was my whistle. It was pretty obvious Lil had no intention of relinquishing her whistle, especially since she'd already charged it with her power. We left Alice and Sylvia clinging to their bench, as an influx of Japanese tourists arrived, making the shallow resting place feel overcrowded.

We continued our descent into the wooded gorge at a much faster pace, making it even more obvious to me that a majority wanted this to be over and done with as soon as possible. The winding staircase of rock and steel went on and on, small level platforms at intervals the only reprieve from the constant twisting, stepping-down motion of our bodies. Sally was the one doing the most moaning now, albeit in a more resigned way. Moving closer to her, I tried to be helpful by repeating the advice of not looking down. She turned on me with an energy fuelled by fear, 'I have to look down, I'm wearing bloody varifocals, and if I don't look down I'll end up over the edge.'

Eventually we reached the valley floor with sighs of relief, instead of the expected smiles of achievement. A daunting dilemma was now waiting to be addressed. I wanted to turn left and fulfil my desire to see the waterfalls. Sally, June and Carol, wanted to turn right and follow the level path which led eventually to the mountain train that would carry them back up to safety and sunshine. Lil couldn't win whatever she decided to do. Sylvia and Alice,

127

clinging to the bench a mile above our heads, couldn't be informed of this by blowing on a whistle.

'Let's just get walking, I'm freezing without my jacket,' said Carol rubbing her arms.

'Oh shit, we haven't got any money with us to pay the train fare, and none of us has got water! What if we have to walk miles?' This was June, realizing that leaving their bags behind was a bad mistake.

'Walk back up the steps then. I'll go with Marg and see you up there later,' reasoned Lil.

'I would rather walk ten miles on the level, than face any more steps; up or down.' This was Sally, standing firm with her arms folded and her lips pressed into a thin line – a line that was turning blue due to the much lower temperature.

Handing round my bottle of water, I noticed that everyone seemed suddenly extra thirsty, and there was a smile of relief as I handed June a fistful of dollars for their train fare. Mindful of her dilemma, I told Lil that I was prepared to make the pilgrimage to the waterfalls on my own. As ever, she wanted to do the right thing by everyone, but you can't split yourself into three, and she wasn't happy about me venturing into the wilds unaccompanied. So after a cheery 'See you later,' she fell into step beside me.

Due to the many months of hot, dry weather, the normally gushing waterfall was now diminished to a babbling spring; no less a beautiful sight, just different than expected. In fact, it reminded me of a section of the small cascading trout stream that ran through a piece of woodland at my home in Devon. No more than a few minutes were spent in its presence; taking a couple of photographs and filling the water bottle. Then we were off, retracing our steps along the myriad of winding paths.

We hadn't chatted much on the way out, I was absorbed in the unfamiliar flora and the variety of huge tree ferns (back home, Barry and I had recently paid a small fortune for a miniscule example). Lil had only one thing on her mind – the clinging pair – and the pace of the return journey, made it obvious that she was concerned. At one point she accidentally diverted onto a wrong path, adding to her frustration and urgency as we almost sprinted back to the bottom of the Devil's Stairway.

'I'll take your bag,' she offered, handing me back the half-drunk bottle of fresh mountain water. Then she disappeared up the first section of the daunting ascent, as nimbly as a ten-year-old.

Barely halfway up and I was already feeling exhausted and acknowledging first hand, why it had been given such an infamous name. My heart was pounding so fiercely I was afraid it might give up on me and my calf muscles were as hard as the rocks I was now desperately trying to mount. Lil was up ahead frantically blowing on her whistle, announcing to the world above that the cavalry were on their way. A piece of wisdom floated down from her between whistle blows, 'Walk sideways up the steps, it's easier on the calf muscles'. Oh blessed relief, it worked. My legs were given a new lease of life, but my heart and lungs were still under immense pressure, causing me to stop more frequently and even question the sanity of doing this.

At one point – in this rail groping effort of an ascent – I raised my head to see Lil grinning down at me from about twenty yards above. She was holding my camera, poised to capture my worst possible state – crawling up the steps on all fours. The whistle blowing had stopped and the fact that she was grinning like a Cheshire cat, meant that she, at least, had reached her goal.

The first resting post came into view – releasing a spurt of energy from some hidden source – that propelled me upward at a faster pace. The shallow cave with its two benches was completely empty. I sat for several minutes in its cool interior, waiting for my breathing and heartbeat to normalise. Lil must have heroically rescued her two sisters, carrying the surplus five bags, single handed, as she led them up to their perceived, safer realm of warm sunshine. A smile creased my face, as I visualised all six of them waiting patiently for me to appear at the top; cameras at the ready to capture the finale of my great achievement. I willed my aching body to stand up straight and mount the final run of steps as a proud human being, instead of the crawling creature I'd become.

There was no welcoming party, in fact there was no one at all to witness the final moments of the most exhausting performance of my life (including giving birth, twice). Alice and Sylvia – their backs toward me – were sitting on yet another bench, still in possession of the pile of bags. But this time they weren't clinging to it and they were in bright sunshine.

After staggering over to them and allowing a few seconds for my lungs to inflate, I asked where Lil was.

'Where do you think, she's gone for a bloody coffee.' Sylvia's cutting response, was blasted forth without any concern for my exhaustion and near collapsed state. Sitting beside them on the bench, my eyes closed against the imminent confrontation, as I allowed my body to gradually relax in the warmth of the sun. I was treated to the one-sided point of view of my two abandoned sisters, who clearly thought that the rest of us had deserted them to swan off and have a bloody good time, whilst they looked after everyone's baggage.

130

'I'll stay here with the bags, why don't you join Lil for a drink?' I offered during a short pause of silence which I mistakenly took for an end to the hostility.

'Drink? do you know 'ow much bloody water we drunk, while perched on that soddin' ledge for over two hours? We drunk every drop from every soddin' bottle – to lighten the bags for carrying up – which meant we were nearly pissing ourselves as we struggled up them soddin' steps.' After this tirade from Sylvia, Alice's softer, anguished voice told how they'd been worried about our safety, and how they'd persistently blown on the whistle but it hadn't worked. I took the whistle from her hand, placed it between my lips and blew as hard as my overworked lungs would allow.

'No, I mean it didn't work because we didn't get an answer from Lil's whistle,' she hissed through clenched teeth, as the glaring eyes of dozens of tourists bore down on us.

Silence descended again. I retreated even further into my own world, searching for the sense of achievement that should have been filling every fibre of my being. I'd successfully accomplished everything I'd set out to do and for the most part, enjoyed doing it. So why this feeling of dissatisfaction? I thought of joining Lil in the café, but found that my body was rebelling as much as my two sisters. I too, became a bench clinger, content to just sit and recuperate beneath the life-giving rays of the sun.

The mountain bus spilled out its passengers, including Sally, June and Carol. They were bright-eyed and smiling until they came close enough to sense the bad vibrations. 'What's up?' asked Carol, with a slight tremble in her voice. I was then treated to a second helping of Alice and Sylvia's tale of woe, with the added input of Sally implying that they had got away very lightly compared to the suffering of herself, June and Carol.

'We felt as vulnerable as lost children walking through a strange jungle and Carol needed the loo, but was too frightened to go behind a bush because of all the poisonous snakes and spiders we'd been warned about.'

Sally's ranting continued, revealing that the consensus of opinion seemed to be that it was all Lil's fault because she knew how difficult the descent was, and for whatever reason, she'd kept that knowledge to herself.

My eyes and mouth had remained closed during this competitive exchange of who had suffered most, but the unfair criticism of Lil – especially when she wasn't present to defend herself – brought me into the fray.

'Look, we all made our choices, now we should bear the consequences and stop bickering. The day's drifting by, let's enjoy it while we can.'

As if on cue, Lil came breezing over to us, a broad smile on her face, showing relief that we were all together again. Five minutes later we were on board the very bus that Sally and co. had just dismounted, travelling to the scenic railway, where five of our number had decided to see for themselves, if there was any truth in Dad's extraordinary tale.

A series of loud screams from across the road grabbed my attention. The screamers were two young women on the back of a Harley Davidson, three-wheeler motor bike. A couple of entrepreneurial guys were hiring out their bikes and riding skills to anyone brave enough to accompany them on a twelve minute speed trip around the narrow mountain lanes. At the beginning and end of each trip a high wheelie was performed, creating the screams of delight, which no doubt were an attraction for anyone else seeking the thrills of speed. The open-terraced café opposite the motor-bike stand had provided me and Sylvia with a place to wait for our sisters' return from their own speed trip – via the world's steepest railway. Before too long they reappeared with their faces intact and an air of disappointment that was unconcealed. A little light refreshment (or dare I say it, comfort food) was agreed on, as the calories of the overlarge breakfast had long since been used up.

Another set of squeals, accompanied by the roar of a powerful engine, attracted even more attention and Alice – who was sitting next to me – said, quite seriously, 'I shouldn't mind a go on that.' Sylvia, who had been very quiet since the earlier dispute, suddenly found her voice, 'You'll never get me on that thing, so don't bother trying.' Alice looked dejected, knowing that two passengers were required for each trip.

'I'll join you Alice,' I said. It did look a bit nerve-racking but hey, I'd just conquered the Devil's Stairway – the up and the down of it. Her beaming smile and childlike excitement made it well worth the challenge

The last time I'd seen Alice on a motor bike was back in the 1950's when she'd first met her husband-to-be, George. It was a great thrill for her siblings to hear and then see him arrive on his powerful machine - young and handsome in his dark suit and tie and well-greased hair (no helmets then), and to watch him sit astride the purring set of wheels, proudly waiting for his pretty, petite Alice. A summer's day image is still clear in my memory, of how she climbed aboard behind him, her full-skirted dress creating colourful wings for the dark, heavy body of the bike, as they zoomed off; with Alice squeezing George's waist in fond delight.

133

'I'm game, it looks more exciting than the train ride,' said June. Several heads looked away from her, then looked back, relieved, when Lil said that she would join her.

Alice and I watched as June and Lil were belted securely in the back seat of the bright, yellow trike. They each wore a black helmet – enclosing face as well as head – and were offered black, leather jackets that were rejected, due to the warm temperature. We stood, cameras at the ready, to capture the optimum moment of the departing, high wheelie; performed now to an even larger audience. The queue had started to swell. The departure of two squealing, middle-aged women and two more waiting in line, had no doubt attracted the curiosity of the milling tourists and an excited murmuring rippled through the crowd.

Several older people wandered over to read the detail on the advertising fly sheet and decided that they too, would take advantage of the thrill on offer, swelling the queue even more. One middle-aged tourist pushed forward and asked if she could go first, as she was in a hurry. Alice straightened her five-foot stature and squared up to the large heavily built woman. 'Yes, well, we're in a hurry too, there's the back of the queue,' and she flicked her hand in true thumbing-a-lift style.

As he double checked the security of our safety belts our rider chatted amiably, indicating his warm personality and the pleasure he gained from his chosen way to earn a crust. We also declined the offer of the leather jackets, the large helmets were already adding to the late afternoon temperatures of 75 degrees. When he was completely satisfied that we were comfortable and secure, with a broad, knowing grin he mounted the front end of the bike saying, 'You can hold hands if you want to.' We looked at him with raised eyebrows concealed under the heavily-hooded helmets, but as he took flight into the first high wheelie, we grabbed each others hands and held on that way throughout the twelve minute ride.

There are some experiences that can't be expressed in words alone, and during the next few minutes time seemed to hold its breath as a rush of exhilaration and sense of freedom lifted us into a higher sphere of consciousness, rendering conversation superfluous. The dramatic panoramic views passed at tremendous speed as we travelled along half-hidden roads that no mountain bus could hope to negotiate, were truly awesome. We were joined by hand and mind in a revelling thrill and at the risk of sounding juvenile, it was magic.

The late afternoon melted into evening and the last bus was waiting to take us back to where we would find our all-inclusive lift to the motel. We were all tired from the hard physical exercise, but the pure mountain air tempered this fatigue with a healthy glow. The unexpected bonus of the high speed scenic tour, on the back of a Harley Davidson, had notched up my achievements to a satisfying level. Alice, I could tell, was still buzzing from her nostalgic reunion with a powerful motorbike, and all her earlier hostility – being abandoned for two hours – was wiped out in twelve short minutes. Sylvia was still a little subdued, but I knew that after eating a hearty, three-course meal with a few glasses of whatever took her fancy, the usual, naturally funny personality would rise again to entertain us in the communal lounge of the motel; provided we could stay awake.

16

Lil and I were already halfway through our breakfast
when Alice and Sally sauntered into the dining room to join
us – both dressed in red and white England tee shirts. The
ear-splitting screech produced by the chair opposite being
dragged out and the contemptuous look at my pale green top
told me that I, at least, was in for some flak.

'Don't you know what day it is?' asked Sally, with a look
that registered both hurt and disappointment. I tried without
success to remember, hoping against hope that I hadn't
inadvertently agreed to take part in some sporting event –
especially as this was our last full day of the mountain trip.

'Saturday?' I answered, trying not to sound too flippant.

'It's St George's Daaay', she came back tartly, hoping
that the lengthening of the word day would hit home its
importance. But apart from feeling that she might at any
moment frogmarch me back to my room – to change into
something containing the colours red and white – I felt a
sweet relief that the day would at least be free from ball
kicking. Lil was obviously regarded as a full-bloodied Ozzie
because no remarks were aimed at her.

June, Sylvia and Carol arrived for breakfast, oblivious of
this sacred day. June had a hint of red and white in her top,
but I think this was more by accident than design. She also
carried dark, heavy bags under her eyes which marred her
usually fresh, pretty face. When asked if she'd slept well, I
wasn't surprised to be told that the previous two nights had
been disastrous for sleep, due to the busy highway.

'It's not just the noise,' she complained, 'the worst thing
is the strobe lighting that cuts across my face from every
vehicle that passes and I see it even with my eyes closed.'

'Why didn't you ask to be moved to a room at the back, the motels half empty so I'm sure it wouldn't have been a problem?' I said sympathetically.

'Because we wouldn't have a balcony,' answered Sylvia in a manner which inferred this was an obvious reason to anyone with half a brain.

'Well I'd rather have a good night's rest, than the occasional sit on a balcony that doesn't look out on anything more scenic than a busy highway. Besides, there hasn't been much opportunity in our busy itinerary (I glanced sideways at Lil) to indulge in just sitting and enjoying a view.'

'What Sylvia means is that the balcony is my smoking room.' June said coyly.

Leura Village, stop number eighteen on the tour bus, is the shopping capital of the mountains and it was here that we had planned to spend the largest portion of our day, hoping to diminish or completely obliterate the remaining names on our lists of presents for taking back to England.

Our trusted motel lift dropped us in Katoomba, with forty-five minutes to spare before the arrival of the mountain bus, so after synchronising watches we split into smaller groups and started our shopping escapade here along its High Street, arranging to meet back at the bus stop within the allotted time.

The thirty minute ride to Leura Village should have been spent enjoying the sites and views – pointed out by the cheerful tour guide – instead, we inspected each others purchases accompanied by a loud rustle of carrier bags being opened and passed around. However, one piece of information did filter through this pre-occupation when he mentioned the emotive words 'two for the price of one.'

Bygone Beauties – a smart tea shop/antique emporium – which reputedly housed a staggering teapot collection of three and a half thousand, was offering Devonshire style cream teas, at two for the price of one. Five of us decided to take advantage of this opportunity and prepare for the next round of shopping by consuming calorie-laden edibles.

The cream teas were superb. Home-made scones – still warm from baking – were served with generous amounts of strawberry jam and clotted cream; every bit as tasty as the fare sold in the best tea shops of my adopted home county. The loose leaf tea – so much more flavoursome than teabags – was particularly enjoyed, served in pretty, bone china cups and saucers. The gentility of the place held us in its spell, causing us to linger longer than we'd planned, but eventually, content with our photographs as a future reminder, we carefully squeezed our enlarged stomachs through the narrow aisles of expensive antiques.

Leura Village, with its large variety of designer-clothes boutiques and high quality craft shops, was testimony to the popularity of this busy mountain tourist attraction. You could spend days in its tempting embrace, provided you had the wherewithal to finance it. But just like in England, provided you were prepared to seek them out there were always several charity shops to be found, and it was in one of these establishments that we met up with Sylvia and Carol.

'Look at this beautiful top for only two dollars, I've seen one almost identical up the road for sixty dollars.' Carol's excitement lit up her face as she held the pretty top against her. Even if it hadn't been particularly special, it would have looked good on her. She had the perfect figure and face to guarantee a second glance whatever she wore. Sylvia and Carol had declined the cream tea in order to get a head start on bargain hunting and they'd started with the high brow charity shops. Not wanting to miss out, we all joined in the rummaging.

On my previous visit to the mountains Lil and I had accidentally stumbled onto a small art gallery, while searching for shelter from a spell of miserable damp weather. We ended up spending a whole afternoon in its tranquil surroundings, where we fell in love with a couple of etchings and after a little soul-searching, decided to each purchase one.

I'd broached the subject at breakfast, implying that I wouldn't mind visiting the place again. The response to my implication was… well there was no response, so I figured I'd have to go alone if I wanted to get a second look around the place. Fortunately for me, by early afternoon Lil had also had enough of shopping and agreed to join me. So after arranging to meet the others back at the motel we jumped in a taxi. There was no time to waste waiting for buses.

The gallery is run by a *husband and wife partnership*, and both are accomplished artists in their own right. Its setting – amid mature woodland gardens – appears very English until you catch sight of the many colourful parrots that are obviously attracted to this sylvan setting; and no doubt encouraged to delight the visitors.

It was very gratifying to be here again, admiring the latest creations of the in-house artists. The etching I'd previously bought myself, had been added to by Lil – as a surprise gift – on one of her frequent visits to England. The two related pieces hang side by side in my dining room, giving immense pleasure each time I study them.

We wandered slowly through the rooms of paintings, etchings and ceramics serenaded by low-volume, classical music – enhancing the already relaxed ambience of the place.

Even Lil's hyperactivity dropped several notches when we walked through the peaceful gardens, taking photographs of the parrots that seemed to pose on cue. We helped ourselves to tea and coffee included in the small entrance fee. Nothing was purchased this time, but a feeling of relaxation and replenished vitality – a priceless commodity of this day and age – was gained free of charge.

The late afternoon sunshine and the neighbouring well-attended gardens encouraged us to walk back to the motel and for the first time on this trip I became visually aware that it was autumn here in Australia. The incandescence of gold, red and amber leaves shimmering above us in the sun laden breeze, was truly a sight to behold.

The motel was filled to capacity with weekenders making the most of the unseasonably warm weather. Live music was included on the Saturday evening menu and as usual, where music and dancing is promised, we girls really dress for the occasion. It was our first opportunity to flaunt the new tops we'd bought at Hurstville, worn with the colourful necklaces and earrings that we'd managed to secure from the tempting places in Leura. This was our last evening at the motel and a determination to make it extra special was everyone's main aim.

Due to the swollen number of guests, there was a much longer gap between courses. Unfortunately, the number of waiters hadn't been swollen, altering their usually sedate manner to a frantic pace of charging around and trying – but not always succeeding – to please. As well as the extra workload, they had to diplomatically deal with several impatient guests, none of which I'm happy to say, were from our table. I felt sorry for the waiters, but I wasn't about to dwell on it, nor allow it to impinge on the lovely voice of the

140

lone singer, strumming his guitar and trying his best to create a soothing balm of melody and song.

Eventually everybody was fed to capacity. Slowly an air of relaxation descended on the dining room – no doubt helped by the copious amounts of alcohol, imbibed whilst waiting for the food. As the tempo of the music increased, several younger guests – with digestive powers stronger than ours – took to the cleared space provided and preceded to gyrate in unison. It wasn't too long before we were all caught up in the same musical spell, especially as the singer moved into the timeless songs of the sixties.

Unbeknown to me it had been decided (probably whilst I was lost in the melodious voice of the lone singer) to seek out one of the clubs in Wentworth later in the evening. The consensus of opinion being: it was bound to be livelier than a motel and the entertainment would go on for much longer. Personally, I was really enjoying myself here. It was interesting to be absorbed into the company of my fellow dancers who were from various, far flung corners of the globe leading me to mimic some of their more interesting dance routines – not caring that I undoubtedly looked 'a bit of a prat'. But as this was our final evening of the highland trip why not add a few extra hours of fun via a heaving night club.

'Well this is very lively and exciting,' I said, trying not to sound too sarcastic. We were sitting around a double table, in the only club we could find that was open. True, there were several people about the place, but they were the remains of a larger group of drinkers who, as we entered, were already breaking up and leaving. There was no live music, in fact there was no music at all, save for the melodic chink of glasses and soft conversational laughter between friends. It

141

was pretty obvious that the best entertainment was back at the motel, but no one actually voiced these words – although Sylvia came pretty close: 'Christ, its only 'alf past ten, what's wrong with these country bumpkins?' But as it turned out, the light-hearted conversation that developed between us (and went on for God knows how long) produced an engaged companionship that would have been overwhelmed by music and dancing.

As Sylvia temporarily broke this engagement to use the loo, we realised that we were the only ones left in the softly lit clubhouse. The one remaining barman was unnecessarily wiping down the gleaming counter, accompanied with a few loud coughs. It wasn't a long walk back to the motel, but not everyone was happy with this mode of travel, especially at this late hour. Sally, who was adamant about not walking – and to emphasise the point, rubbed her still aching legs from her nightmarish descent of the Devil's Stairway – approached the barman wearing her broadest smile. He, in turn, looked relieved at the chance to be off and promptly offered a lift to three of our number – Sally, Alice and Sylvia – instead of ringing for a taxi, which he was probably well aware, didn't always turn up.

The air was balmy and perfumed and the gentle stroll back was far more pleasant than the frantic march of our arrival. The traffic was much lighter too, giving Carol the opportunity to fill the quietness with her rendition of, 'Is this the way to Amarillo?' sung much more softly when I told her of the barking dog we'd encountered along this way.

The motel was locked and in total darkness when we arrived back. Thankfully, Lil had retained the knowledge of which keys to use, on which doors, when arriving back after a certain time. The three of our number that had ridden back were safely in the motel, hovering to make sure that we too, arrived safely. With genuine affection we bid each other good night, trying our very best to creep to our rooms without developing the giggles and disturbing our fellow guests.

17

Very much aware that time was eating its way into our
trip of a lifetime at an alarming rate, we planned the day
ahead with Lilian-like precision. George was arriving around
midday to provide the extra car space needed to transport us
all back to Sydney. This gave us several hours to fill with
whatever took our fancy. It was agreed, that after our usual
hearty breakfast, we would vacate our rooms and leave all
the luggage locked in Lil's car at the motel car park. Our
chosen fancy was to visit a Sunday Market in Katoomba,
making good use – for the final time – of the concessionary
motel lift. This would no doubt swallow up the morning; and
a taxi to return us back in time to meet up with George would
swallow up a little more of our fast dwindling cash – but that
couldn't be helped.

The second part of our chosen fancy required the agreed
participation of George, and the task of coercing him would
be left in Lil's capable hands. By early evening we would
arrive at our new motel, with plenty of time to unpack and
settle in for the last week of our Australian holiday.

The Sunday Market (which was really a car boot sale)
was situated at the lower end of Katoomba; an urban area
that we hadn't had cause to use until now. We'd all seen the
fly sheets advertising the market, but no one had thought it
necessary to memorise the address! So it took a little while
and a few helpful directions from the locals, to locate the
open space that housed the dozen or so vehicles. Apart from
one or two exceptions, the owners of these vehicles were
selling household items accumulated over the years and no
longer needed – or, were never wanted in the first place.

I headed for one of the two exceptions. Two, six-foot-long
tables were placed end to end forming a generous area where

semi-precious stones, shaped crystals and an impressive amount of fossils were displayed. At least forty-five minutes was spent sifting through the neatly, labelled polythene bags from the section of the table marked Ancient Curios. I was hoping to find a fossil or fossil-imprint of a fish, small lizard or even a more common invertebrate, provided it was of Australian origin. Nothing came to light that I felt would be a suitable present for my husband. But I didn't come away from that stall completely empty handed, and the three interestingly carved crystals that I did purchase, took up just a miniscule amount of space in my purse.

There wasn't much buying going on from our group we were all too mindful of the impending struggle to carry everything home to England. But it was an enjoyable Sunday morning activity, wandering from car to car, witnessing first-hand the good-natured bartering between the native Australians.

We knew this leisurely pace was about to change when we saw Lil moving closer to the exit and continuously looking at her watch. Like a well-trained sheep dog, she was about to draw in her flock and guide us back to our next rendezvous.

As I rode down the busy highway towards Sydney, alongside Lil and behind George's gleaming white saloon car, my mind indulged in fantasies conjured up whilst thinking of our next destination. Lil had succeeded in getting George to agree to visit a wildlife park that was conveniently situated just off the highway en route to Sydney. Apart from parrots and the odd cockroach, none of us had seen any Australian wildlife, so here was the best opportunity to remedy this.

145

George's face had taken on some odd expressions whilst Lil was doing the coercing, but none of us were close enough to hear what was being said – deliberately keeping a safe distance from any verbal fallout. The whole group of us (except maybe George) were excited to be heading for a real Australian safari.

So as to blend with the surroundings I wore my beige bush shorts, boots and a pale green top, with my hat to hand for the possible patient wait. Camouflaged amongst the sparse flora I envisaged the unrolling scenario of wild kangaroo or wallaby, eagerly caught on camera. My fantasies danced around a mixture of Jurassic Park, Skippy the bush Kangaroo and Picnic at Hanging Rock.

My fantasies started to evaporate as we drove into the compound of the wildlife park. Its numerous cages and pens, at the point of entry, holding creatures sadly resigned to their fate, didn't dispel my hopes completely. Maybe beyond lay the open parkland, where kangaroo roamed and koala slept, half hidden in Eucalyptus trees. But the reality fully hit home as the 'Passport Admission Map' was given to each of us to study.

We were entering a touchy-feely place for children encouraged and guided via the passport map, to each section of species; where they could watch, touch and even feed the animals on display. The passport could be stamped at each section; proof that the child had in fact been present. Whether he or she had gained any knowledge from the experience was in the lap of the Gods.

The more dangerous wildlife, such as crocodiles, snakes and spiders, were kept in more secure housing, still just about visible for the collective entertainment of the more toughened, thrill-seeking kids, but not conducive for taking photos. As it was, you would need to employ some very nifty photographic skills to capture any of the animals for posterity, without the intrusion of wire caging, or the body parts of small human beings that were constantly reaching and pointing between camera and creature.

For the umpteenth time I tried to photograph Lil alongside a marching emu which was desperately trying to escape a young boy, whose intention was to mount the bird and ride on its back. I pulled him away a couple of times; explaining that the bird didn't like it and might kick him in response. His watching mother glared at me for daring to consider a mere bird in preference to her beloved son.

We each waited in line to have our photograph taken stroking a koala bear that slept through the spoken endearments and the many prodding fingers. This oblivion to the daily molestation was created by its sleep-inducing diet of eucalyptus leaves. Every now and then the small bear would urinate, to the whooping delight of any young boy who happened to witness the event. In fact, a small group of youngsters seemed to spend the whole of their schools allotted time engrossed in this one spasmodic occurrence.

George hung back from it all, not wanting to take any photographs; in fact not wanting to be here at all. I wandered over to him at one point and asked if he was ready for a bite to eat. The horrified look on his face made the following words unnecessary.

'There's no way I'm eating here!'

'Come on then, I'll treat you to a coffee,' I continued encouragingly. His eyes swept over the busy café area that was filled with children satisfying their lunchtime hunger.

'Nope,' was his simple reply. I understood his game plan; which was probably one of the conditions for bringing us here: there was to be no time wasted on eating or drinking.

Heaven forbid it might rejuvenate us all for a second run of passport stamping. I also understood now why he was standing in front of the café with arms folded and a determined look on his face. I was starting to feel very hungry, but I knew that the bottle of water and the few pieces of leftover liquorice, concealed in my bag, were the only sustenance I could expect before reaching Sydney.

We were all ravenous by the time we reached Sydney and located a café happy to cook meals at this late afternoon hour. Everything sounded good as several excited voices read aloud from the wall-mounted blackboard. I decided on Lamb Shanks, the first meal I'd ordered containing red meat, since landing in this hot climate country. It was cooked to perfection and every scrap of the enormous meal was eaten with relish. To round off, we all shared a large fondue bowl of chocolate sauce and marshmallows, laughing as we dipped and dripped the melted chocolate on the table, reminding me of the happy hordes of children back at the zoo.

Three of us struggled with the luggage of six up the wide, carpeted staircase of our new motel. Lil and George had already left to drive home and return with the remainder of the suitcases they'd been storing for us. Alice and Sally had dashed on ahead to locate the room and open up. And by the time I reached this room – breathless with exertion – the door was wide open showing each of them perched on the bed of their choice.

'I've bagged this bed, Marg,' announced Alice, sitting proudly on a queen bed. It was flanked by two enormous bedside cabinets that incorporated inset lighting and a multi-purpose remote control. Behind her was a pile of plumped up pillows, to add support for that bedtime read that I hadn't yet been able to enjoy.

Sally was sitting on the single bed next to her, arms spread out to enforce the gesture that this was her territory. She too, would have a share of the luxurious, bedside cabinet and to draw my attention to this fact, she plonked her handbag down on it saying, 'My Space.'

The remaining single bed, with its one pillow, no headboard or light, was pushed up against the full length window giving a fifteen-inch gap of nothing, between it and Sally's bed. This was my allotted space for the final week of our holiday. I felt a deep sense of hurt at the injustice of this decision, made in my absence and whilst struggling with their luggage. Ok, I was the youngest and a certain pecking order always exists between kids in large families. But we're not kids anymore, we're all grandmothers for God's sake and looking back, I recall most democratic decisions were made at the toss of a coin – provided we could lay our hands on one.

Only two minutes into our posh motel and I was feeling really pissed off. I'd spent most of this trip calming the troubled waters between one sister and another; but I'll be damned before I take this lying down! I tried – not very diplomatically – to communicate my hurt feelings, but they continued to mark 'their' territory with personal items from their handbags and even clothes off their backs – because most of their belongings were in that bloody suitcase I'd just struggled to carry. Back in the aeons of time, man marked his territory in a much more personal way, as animals today. I tried to gain a little comfort from that thought.

Resigned to my fate, I dropped the portion of luggage that was mine onto the vacant bed, leaving the rest outside. I grabbed one of the three chairs that were positioned around

149

an outside table and crammed it – with more force than was needed – between mine and Sally's bed. At least I'd have a surface on which to place my watch and a glass of water. I'd given up all hope of reading. The four days spent at the mountain motel were ideal for bedtime reading. Unfortunately, my ability to comprehend the writings at the end of those exhausting days, was far from ideal.

My eyes swept around the room taking in everything that wasn't attached to the queen bed. A fixed counter ran along the entire length of the room facing the beds, and below this counter were four long drawers and several cupboards. The nearest of these two long drawers were quickly commandeered and filled with underwear, beachwear and casual tops – a task normally executed with care and pleasure – but on this occasion done at break-neck speed, leaving bits of underwear trapped in the closed drawer front.

I opened the wardrobe and removed two of the six pathetic-looking coat hangers, holding them close to my person as I moved into the shower area. Here, I spread out my small array of toiletries, making absolutely sure that they covered one third of the available space. Propelled by revenge, I was first to finish unpacking. I could have made us all a welcoming cup of tea, but instead I walked to the far end of the outside corridor to see how the other three were faring.

Determined not to be given the short straw for a third time, June had secured the queen bed – even though she had been one of the stronger three carrying the luggage. Although I was pleased to see her victorious, a nagging doubt throbbed at the back of my adrenalin-overloaded brain. June is the oldest of these three younger sisters of mine, so how come the natural pecking order had only just kicked in?

150

I was forced to admit that it's all down to individual personalities – who could be pushy – versus who could be pushed.

A strange intermittent rumble made my throbbing head feel worse and brought an abrupt end to my analysis of the given situation.

'Sounds like you've got an air blockage in the plumbing system,' I said, walking over to turn the tap on in the shower area.

'It's that soddin' road,' said Sylvia distractedly, as she folded clothes into her portion of a large cupboard.

This room – it turned out – was about twenty yards away from one of the busiest arterial roads that led into Sydney, and the noise produced from it, was far worse than the mountain highway. I found it hard to believe that all three were happily unpacking, knowing that they'd have to cope with that awful noise every night they were here.

'Why don't you demand a room in a quieter position, the motel is almost empty,' I said, feeling very pushy and prepared to accompany anyone to reception. June looked at the queen bed already marked with her personal items and declined my offer, saying that she was sure she could get used to the traffic noise. It amazed me how different we were in some respects and how alike in others. I wandered back to my own room hoping to find a fresh pot of tea.

By nine thirty Lil and George had been and gone; all the unpacking was done and the three of us were in bed testing our new sleeping positions. To have been able to read, I would've had to insist on keeping the bright light on that was situated dead centre of the ceiling, and I, being the insister, would have had to get out of bed to turn it off. Fortunately for everyone, I was far too tired to want to do either, preferring to lay down in the soft glow of Alice's bedside light, as she flicked through her magazine.

Sally was already making her soft animal noises when a tapping on the door meant someone needed to get out of bed to answer it. I saw Alice look over to where I lay motionless. This end of the room was in shadow, so I knew she couldn't tell if I was asleep or not. A more urgent tapping dragged her from her high status position amongst the plumped up pillows with a heavy sigh and soft, inaudible mutterings.

Sylvia's voice, loud and unmistakable, filled our quiet room – even though she was standing outside the open door. She was informing us – in her usual long winded, round the houses way – that she, June and Carol had decided to have a couple of drinks at the motel bar before turning in and would we like to join them? I remained motionless, determined not to be coerced out of bed for anything, except the need to empty my bladder, which I could now sense was rapidly filling to danger-level.

Suddenly, Sally sat bolt upright in mid snore and shouted, 'Shut up!' A shocked silence descended on the room. I forgot my pretence at being asleep and asked her if she was having a bad dream. 'Yes,' she said loudly, 'I dreamt Sylvia was shouting in my ear 'ole.'

We heard three pairs of footsteps receding in the direction of reception, as all the lights were turned out and good nights were exchanged. I nipped to the bathroom in the soft, orange glow of an outside security light, thinking that this at least was very handy for a middle of the night trip to the loo.

152

18

'Far be it from me to spoil everyone's day, but the in-house cooked breakfast that we've become used to having, and thought was going to continue whilst we were here, apparently isn't available; not today, tomorrow, nor the following two days; and even worse – there is absolutely no way we can buy any food today to counteract this.'

'Ya what?' said Sally, poised halfway through pouring a cup of tea from the teapot. 'Talk proper, bloody English,' she continued, with a mixture of irritation and trepidation.

After a good night's sleep I'd woken early, taken a shower and dressed, feeling particularly pleased that I'd managed to achieve this without waking either of my sisters. With time to spare, I wandered down to reception to find out about breakfast times and menus.

After having our breakfasts conveniently provided over the last four days, we'd all decided that for the final week of our holiday we would sod the expense and do away with the self-catering malarkey altogether. The motel would provide breakfasts (not inclusive with the price of the room unfortunately) and we would rely on café's and restaurants for our other meals. All in all the cost of eating out in Australia was so reasonable it wasn't worth the effort of shopping, cooking and washing up.

It was surprisingly quiet at reception; an attractive looking young woman, casually flicking through a magazine, was the only sign of life. Although it was past eight o'clock, the expected clatter of a kitchen in preparation for breakfasts was missing, as were any signs of people, like myself, looking forward to being fed.

On voicing my concern to the attractive young woman I was informed that breakfast is only served on Fridays,

Saturdays and Sundays and she finished with a bright smiling 'Didn't you know?'

I bit my tongue and asked, with as much equanimity as I could muster, where was the nearest café? The bright smile returned as I was further informed that all café's and indeed all stores would be closed, because today was ANZAC Day – a public bank holiday. She annoyingly ended once again, with the words 'Didn't you know?'

This time, afraid that I might do something far worse than biting my tongue, I turned tail and went back up the carpeted stairs that led to our room.

'Do the others know? They were in the bar last night, they must have heard something,' enquired Sally, trying to come to terms with this devastating news.

'I'll go down and see June when I've drunk my tea, she's bound to be aware of the situation,' I offered, reaching out for the cup of brown liquid barely recognisable as tea, because only one thimble-size milk carton remained to share between the three of us.

Lil had naturally told us about ANZAC (Australia and New Zealand Army Corps) a proud day in the Australian calendar. What she hadn't told us was that there was a good chance we'd all be on an enforced fast for this celebrated day.

'We've got a big bag of anorak biscuits that Lil left us, so we won't starve,' said Alice spookily reading my mind and doing her best to ease the situation.

'It's ANZAC not anorak!' I corrected her.

'Well they still taste the same,' she responded, throwing one over to where I sat on the bed.

As if by telepathy June knocked on our door to confirm what I had already been told at reception. She went on to say that the three of them, after having one drink at the almost

154

empty motel bar, went on a walkabout looking for shops (I think she meant bars), but in the direction that they'd headed, neither was found.

'Let's take a walk in the opposite direction,' I suggested to Alice and Sally, who were now showered and dressed. I'd remembered seeing a small group of shops down the highway at the first set of traffic lights, as we'd arrived the evening before.

Forty-five minutes later we were back clutching bread, cereals, orange juice and unripe bananas, plus two sets of coat hangers. The store where we'd bought these precious commodities was owned by a non-Australian. He'd decided to open for a few hours in the morning to accommodate the less organised people of this area, giving them a chance to pop in and buy the odd forgotten item. Between the three of us we must have said the word thank you at least a dozen times before leaving his store. As we passed the other closed business outlets, we took particular notice of what they were selling. A bottle shop, newsagents, hairdressers and most importantly a small café, would thankfully all be trading as normal the next day.

The motel rooms were not equipped for self-caterers. A kettle, teapot, three cups and saucers – with teaspoons – were the only utensils available. A few tea bags, miniscule portions of milk and three packets of biscuits – each containing two biscuits per packet, were the only refreshments on offer – and these had mostly disappeared within an hour of arriving yesterday.

The continuous rumbling of my stomach added a determination to the necessary task, as I headed once again to reception, accompanied this time by June. Wearing my sweetest smile and broadcasting a warm and friendly 'Hi,' to the young attractive receptionist, I explained our dilemma, emphasizing that without her help, we had no means of providing for an independent breakfast. I was tempted to finish with, 'Didn't you know?' but instead I smiled expectantly. Thankfully the charm worked. She unlocked the kitchen room and gave us carte blanche to take what we needed. The folded carrier bag that had been concealed in the palm of my hand was hastily filled with packets of butter, jams and milk, plus enough crockery and cutlery to allow for any future, unforeseen circumstance. Taking care that the receptionist was fully occupied with her magazine, June slipped up the carpeted stairs with the bag, whilst I walked over to her counter holding a few token items in my hand, thanking her most profusely.

'I think were lost,' announced Sally, shifting her shoulder bag to a more comfortable position. We were making our way through the vast park that bordered the waters edge to meet up with Carol, Alice and Sylvia. After our impromptu breakfast, they had gone on ahead – using a more direct route – to meet up with Lil and George as prearranged the evening before. The plan was to spend several relaxing hours by the waters edge enjoying what thousands of other families would be doing today – picnicking. The problem was, the only contribution we could provide for a picnic was a bag of ANZAC biscuits. So Sally, June and I had offered to remedy this by taking a detour to the Non-Australian store for more supplies.

This offer had proved to be a bad idea. The store was closed and we were now faced with a much longer walk, in an area that was unfamiliar to us. Burdened with beach towels, water and all the paraphernalia for picnicking (bar the food), we trudged steadfastly across the park towards the distant, glittering water; which was glimpsed every now and then through the trees.

'Where the bloody 'ell are we?' gasped Sally, as we emerged from the trees to join a well walked section of a coastal path.

'I'm sure when we round the next bend we'll see where we need to be.' I was pondering over the deep cut in the coastline that was causing all the extra walking and my words didn't sound very convincing. The morning was developing into another hot day, the earlier mist having been burnt off unnoticed, while we were preoccupied with the more mundane needs of life. The three of us were hot and tired and Sally, who was also worried and agitated, was suffering the most.

'I see them!' shouted June, pointing to a group of bodies nestled amongst a stand of trees just back from the waters edge. It was only when we got much closer that I could determine each individual and what they were doing. A card game was being played between Sylvia and Carol, with the remaining three people happily watching.

'I'm not playing cards or watching it being played,' I said, dropping my burden on the sand several yards from the card game, eager to do one thing only – strip down to my bikini and go for a swim. Sally's relief was obvious and so was her intention. She grabbed the oversized rubber ring from Alice's side and joined June and I at the water's edge. We splashed and paddled about up to our thighs, allowing our overheated bodies to adjust to the cooler temperatures of the ocean, only dimly registering the slick, unpleasant feel underfoot and the tendrils of weed that tickled our legs.

Dozens of children played on the half-grassed, half-sandy slopes of the shoreline, but strangely, none were tempted into the sparkling water. In fact one little boy was being dragged

and scolded by his mother for daring to jump into the
shallow edge, mimicking our frolics. As on most popular
Australian beaches, shark nets were positioned in a wide arc
across the bay, so it wasn't the fear of a marauding shark that
had prompted the mother's wrath.

The light-hearted chatter and laughter of Sally's voice
receded, as she sat comfortably on her rubber throne, bum
touching water, arms and legs dangling over its edge. June
wasn't doing much talking, because it was her swimming
that propelled the two of them out towards the shark net. Not
being able to keep up with June's powerful strokes, I stopped
to rest awhile. The water level came up to my chin but within
seconds my head was dragged below water, as several inches
of mud and weeds sucked and held my lower limbs captive
in their slimy embrace. A surge of adrenalin, laced with
panic, provided enough impetus for me to surface, kicking
and choking.

Looking across the water beyond where the shark net cut
a black serrated line across its undulating, shimmering
surface, I could just make out the ghostly images of distant
buildings. The dawning realisation that we were swimming
in an estuary turned my panic into cold, trembling fear,
eating into the dwindling energy reserves of my body. I cast
my eyes around for any possible help. There was none. June
and Sally had headed diagonally across the water to where
the shark net met the shore, putting even further distance
between us. Provided I could summon the energy to swim
back to shore I'd be fine. But what I couldn't do – if I was to
live to tell the tale – was allow my legs to touch bottom
again. Panic took hold again as I watched the bobbing shape
of my sisters, completely unaware of the danger that lay
beneath them and too far away for me to shout a warning. I
reasoned that my best hope – for all our sakes – was to swim

out to the shark net, where at least I could rest a while. Then I could wave, shout or do whatever it took to attract their attention, hoping in the meantime that Sally didn't accidentally fall from her life-saving perch.

Kicking out in the direction of deeper water, every breath of energy and resolve was harnessed and pinpointed on the shark net. As I swam towards it nothing, except the site of that net – moving painfully slowly towards me – was allowed into my thoughts.

The last few yards found me flailing in the water like a non-swimmer and for one awful moment I thought my efforts had been in vain. But after spitting out a mouthful of salt water and a final kick forward, I was holding on to my salvation. I clung to it with arms, legs and feet wrapped around its mesh structure, thanking God for helping me to reach a possible escape from the watery element that I was still suspended in.

Gradually, the slowing rhythm of my breathing quietened, allowing a voice to penetrate the pounding that still filled my head.

'Are you alright Marg?' I heard June shout from some distance away, pushing with her legs as Sally paddled with her hands to propel the rubber ring towards me. I was still too breathless to shout, but a nodding head brought a smile to their worried faces.

'We're going back to shore,' she shouted, and proceeded to paddle along quite sedately on a course parallel to the net, but keeping a short distance from it to protect the rubber ring from puncturing. As I watched them move easily along together I cursed my stupidity for not staying close earlier; all three of us could have happily manoeuvred the rubber ring without needing to pause for breath.

For twenty yards or so I still found it difficult to totally abandon the security of the net, choosing to follow their direction by hand-walking its length, with my legs hanging free. When I did feel strong enough to swim again, I remained as close to its comforting presence as possible. Occasionally – due to distant boats disturbing the water – a large wave would disrupt my rhythm and send me once more clinging full length to the net. It was on such an occasion that June turned and asked once again if I was alright. My face must have reflected the terror I was feeling.

Eventually I felt firm rock beneath my feet and as I scrambled along it to dry land, I doubted whether I'd have the nerve to ever go sea-bathing again.

'Christ what's happened to you?' exclaimed June, looking me up and down. I followed her eyes and saw the countless lacerations across my stomach, arms and legs that formed an interesting criss-cross pattern of weeping, red lines. Testing first for solidity, I stepped back into the shallow edge and splashed the salt water over my scratched body, knowing that nature's fresh air would do the rest.

'Were you attacked by a shark or something?' asked Sally, full of concern.

'No, barnacles,' I said, realising now, but not being aware at the time, that the net must have been covered in them.

Walking around the same deep cut in the coastline that we'd travelled on arrival, was done in silence. The relief I felt from being on dry land masked the terror that still lay just below the surface of consciousness. A couple of times I thought about pouring out the emotion of it to Sally and June, but then chickened out, either because I couldn't quite face the ordeal again – even verbally – or, I was too ashamed to lay my fears bare.

160

We reached the rest of our party, who were still as we had left them, grouped around a pack of cards in silent concentration. Exhausted, I lay face down on my beach towel in the warm dappled sunshine. As I slipped into a twilight state of semi-consciousness, I heard George remonstrating with Sally about the dangers of swimming in the estuary.

'There's deep silt and weed beds out there you know, no one swims in the estuary.'

'Well 'ow are we supposed to know that, we've never been 'ere before?' argued Sally.

19

I awoke from a nightmare that left me bathed in a cold sweat and feeling disorientated. In the soft glow of the outside security light, I tried to recapture its detail before it dissipated and disappeared completely.

A child of no more than five-years-old was suspended in fathomless water, both arms clinging fearfully to the chunky rail at the edge of a chlorinated swimming pool. The child's legs – bent at the knees – were pulled in tight to a chest that pulsated with fearful breathing. Other young children splashed and swam around in the water, encouraging the child to let go and join in their fun. The recognised face of a swimming instructor, reached out his arms to take hold of the child's shoulders in an effort to induce confidence, but the subsequent screams and a tightening grip on the rail, made him turn away in frustration, until eventually, the child was lifted out of the water, shivering and ashamed.

It was obvious who the child was. As well as the swimming instructor, I recognised all the young faces around me; excited about this first visit to the school baths. Even though I was now wide awake, and it was over fifty years ago, I remember that I too had been excited, until the evening prior to the school trip. Tommy, my older brother by two years, had dropped a bombshell by telling me that there was no floor to the swimming pool, 'So if you don't swim, you'll sink and drown,' he'd said mischievously. And on some impressionable, naive level, I must have believed him.

In time I did learn to swim, not in a chlorinated pool with dozens of children splashing about (the smell and noise of such an environment affected me for years), but in a fresh water gravel pit, not far from where we lived. It had been a family outing on a sunny, Sunday afternoon and my Dad, with patience and understanding, gave me the confidence to finally lift my legs from the firm ground underfoot and awkwardly swim my first, few, unaided strokes.

I regard myself to be an average swimmer, preferring the open sea to a chlorinated swimming pool, but I've always felt nervous about being out of my depth and I was beginning to understand why.

The toilet flushed and Alice's night-gowned body came into focus as she passed through a beam of soft light, before disappearing again and climbing into bed; all done with a deftly silence that made me wonder if I was still dreaming. Two minutes later her loud snoring told me that I wasn't. Although I was much more aware and familiar with her sleeping habits, it still amazed me to see how easily she could slip back into sleep, leaving me lying fully awake.

The celebratory day hadn't been a total loss. Lil and George had departed for a meal in the early afternoon. They had asked if we wanted to join them, but I'm sure, were relieved when we'd declined. The restaurant they had in mind was quite posh and although they were both casually dressed they still appeared crisp and clean, with not a hair out of place.

When hunger had started to bite, June and I had confidently set off into the heart of the park, looking for a vendor selling hot food. We skirted one section of the park's vast perimeter, walking across manicured grass where families and friends picnicked and barbequed. There were large and small groups, interspersed with children playing their favourite ball game in the warm afternoon sunshine. I pointed out a middle-aged couple, intimately positioned under a large eucalyptus tree, eating at a small, fold-up table that was set with flowers and lovely tall wine glasses. This sight brought on thoughts of my husband and how much I was looking forward to seeing him again.

It had soon become obvious that nothing was being sold in the park, so we hopped over the perimeter wall onto a busy road, without having a clue where we were. Half an hour later we reached the same enclave of shops that we'd found before breakfast. The food store was still closed, but fortunately a nearby garage, equipped with a small shop for the convenience of motorists, was open.

Six bottles of fruit drinks, pre-packed hot dogs (which were cold and felt disgusting) and several chocolate bars were purchased. A one minute zap in the shop's microwave made the hot dogs piping hot and feeling even more disgusting, but payment had to be made before you were allowed to open the sealed packaging. Hardly the best ingredients for a celebratory picnic, but we'd felt relief that we wouldn't be returning empty-handed. The weight of the goods was split evenly between the two of us before setting off almost at a gallop to feed the family.

My heart had dropped to my boots as we'd returned to the same spot we'd left them. It had been empty of people. But shouts from recognised voices and June's sharp eyesight, soon had us reunited. A sudden shower (can you believe it) had sent them running for cover to an open-sided wooden building furnished with picnic tables. Their contribution was a secured table where we set out our meagre picnic, vowing to make up for that evening, what we'd been denied that day.

The thirst that had plagued me earlier, and was caused by too much alcohol during the evening, was back, only now my glass was empty. I knew that I wouldn't be able to sleep, but it was far too early to rise and be active. Alice and Sally were still fast asleep; proof of this reverberated around our shared room, so as quietly as I could I rose to satisfy my thirst and as added insurance against having to rise again, I visited the loo.

There was a slight chill in the air and as I pulled the blanket up to my chin and settled down again beneath its warmth, the memory of the day before continued to roll like a played back video recording.

We'd walked into the same RSL club that housed the large screen showing Blackburn Rovers play and lose, nine days earlier. It was absolutely packed out with Australians of all ages still celebrating ANZAC day, even though it was almost eight o'clock in the evening.

This club had now become our local – or to be more precise – one of two local clubs that were equidistant to our new motel. We had all become strong walkers, which was just as well, because on this night taxis would be very thin on the ground. Lil, who wasn't joining us this evening, had given us the most direct route to take, cutting through a suburban estate and emerging just a short walk down a familiar main road that led to the club.

The appetizing smell of food had led us straight to the restaurant area where fortunately we'd managed to secure a table large enough for six. We were all starving-hungry and this produced the unprecedented step of ordering food before drinks. Gazing around at our fellow diners we could see that, as usual, the portions were large – matching our appetites – so a variety of oriental-style dishes were decided upon for us to share. Sally had opted out of this share-all, preferring to stick with her favourite – fish and chips.

Once the food order had been sorted, June and Sylvia disappeared to the bar, returning five minutes later with a loaded tray. Five, tall, straight glasses – bubbling with clear liquid – surrounded a single glass of bright orange, Vodka Breezer. My first thought had been aimed at the ransacked kitty purse and how long it could stand the strain of the champagne high life. But I was soon to be comforted by June.

'I can't believe how cheap the drinks are here,' she'd said, bubbling as much as the drink she was handing me.

'That's because I told him we were members,' cut in Sylvia, pleased with her input at keeping costs down. 'Try and get him to serve us every time,' she'd added, then proceeded to glug down the bubbly as fast as drinking her usual glass of beer. On taking my first sip of the drink I'd realised it wasn't champagne. White wine and soda, for some unknown reason, had then become the popular drink of the evening, except for Alice, who had continued with her brightly-coloured vodkas that had cost double the price. I'd lost track of how many we'd consumed. The constant reminder that they were cheap, and the fact that June had taken charge of the kitty purse, had left me somehow, unburdened of responsibility. My only thought had been – I'll suffer for it later.

The food had been excellent and when the bill had arrived, we were all amazed at how inexpensive the meal had been. This had generated the collective will to purchase yet another tray of drinks and to reward the hard-working Chinese waitress (who also happened to be one of the cooks) with an oversize tip.

Gradually the place had become less crowded as families dispersed, taking their overtired children home before they became too fractious. Then the early risers left; no doubt mindful of a good nights rest before work the next day. It wasn't long before we too, were heading for the door,

166

leaving behind just a few late night revellers and a bunch of tired staff.

Loud upbeat music had pulsated from the pub opposite, but after being tempted through its doors, we had found it to be as empty as the club we'd left. Nevertheless we were still enticed into having one more drink. Mine had been a lime and lemonade and thankfully, now that my sisters had come to accept my lower-than-average tolerance to alcohol, there were no longer the good-natured jeers and jibes, although on this particular occasion Sylvia had asked me quite seriously, if I was a lapsed alcoholic.

It hadn't taken long to realise that the loud, upbeat music was for the sole benefit of the bar staff. Clearing tables, rinsing glasses, mopping floors, had all been carried out in perfect timing to the song 'I Will Survive.' No matter the gender, bums wiggled as hands worked and none of them were the least put out that they had been providing us with last-drink entertainment.

Again we'd moved out into the night, this time with the vain hope of flagging down a taxi. No such luck. We'd been told that all taxis would now be gainfully employed in the big city, where partying would continue throughout the night. The presenter of this knowledge was a young guy who had been sitting next to Carol in the club and was now doing his utmost in persuading her to accompany him to such a party.

'There's six of us and were sticking together,' Alice had announced, pushing forward and standing directly in front of him. This had put him off his sweet-talking stride. He'd given Carol a defeated smile and had said in his broad, Australian twang that had complimented his sunburnt, handsome face, 'Sorry love, there's only room for one in my car. Back in a mo',' and he'd disappeared back into the pub.

'He's a really nice guy, I've been talking to him for ages and he's promised to get me back to the motel,' Carol had said all in a rush, looking behind her to see if he was returning. June in a lowered, sympathising voice had said, 'She's much younger than us, she's bound to be missing the late nights and the partying.'

After the hours of walking earlier in the day and the exhausting time spent in the estuary, I ached for my bed. Plus we still had a two-mile walk back. But I swear to God that this had no bearing on my determination to get all six of us moving in the direction of our motel, before a situation developed where we could be split up.

'We're all going home together,' I said firmly, placing my arms around Carol's shoulders.

'Where's the harm in enjoying a bit of fun at a party?' she'd asked, showing a stronger will than usual.

'We'd be letting all our families down if we allowed one of us to go off on their own with a complete stranger, no matter how nice he appears.'

She'd continued to argue that she felt like an old fogey, going home at this early hour, and I argued back that on a Monday night in England she would already be in bed and so would her grown up children. I would have argued with her till the cows came home and when at last she realised this and that the rest of her sisters were in agreement with me, she bid the young man good night and joined us for the walk home.

Differences and disappointments were soon forgotten as we'd strolled down the main road, gazing through the windows of several high class shops. We were thankful that they'd been closed because we had neither the willpower to resist, nor the space in our cases to carry, any items that might have caught our inebriated fancy.

168

As we'd walked through the suburban estate – retracing the route we'd travelled earlier – peels of laughter broke out from behind us, bringing me and June to a halt. Sylvia – urgently needing the loo – had squatted down behind a bush and Alice had crept up behind her with a loaded camera. The subsequent flash coupled with Sylvia's squeals, caused a barking dog and several neighbourhood lights to be turned on, sending Sylvia running for cover with her clothes not quite adjusted.

It was gone midnight when we'd reached the motel. Reception was closed at this late hour so we'd reached our corridor by way of the open-mesh, steel staircase that served as a fire escape. We'd tried our best to be quiet, but the memory of the Devil's Stairway was too much for some, as I heard once again a range of profanities that were thankfully delivered in hushed tones.

In the pre-dawn hour of Tuesday morning my mind was still fully occupied with the aftermath of the previous day's events. The room was now as quiet as the proverbial grave and my physically relaxed body, warm and comfortable, was patiently waiting for it's brain to slip into sleeping mode.

The little grey cells had been overworked analyzing and trying to fully understand the differences in mental outlook between myself and my sisters. After much soul searching I'd come to the conclusion that their philosophy on life was simply to have a good time as often as possible. Whereas mine was…well, more complex…and definitely more uptight. And it was this uptightness that needed to be addressed and relaxed, before the remaining four days slipped away. It was time to make changes, to hang loose, to go with the flow. Even Lil – well known for her stringent organising and fully accepted as the family's Bossy Boots –

was more laid back than me, showing her bright white smile and taking stress in her stride wherever and whenever it arose.

Having given up on sleep, I decided to wait ten more minutes before rising and putting on the kettle. A new day was dawning; perfect for starting my new – don't worry, be happy – way of life.

20

The ten minute wait, turned out to be one hour twenty minutes of dream-free, restorative sleep. This unexpected, but very welcome start to the first day – as a more laid-back woman – confirmed that I was indeed, on the right path to personal development.

Sally was already up and busying about with tea cups, as Alice blow-dried her washed hair.

'Good morning,' I proclaimed, with an over joyous air, pinning back a broad smile and deftly nipping out of bed. Sally looked in my direction for a split second, before saying accusingly, 'Those bloody white wine and sodas have given me a bad head.'

My personal plan for the day (and hopefully for the rest of my life, once I'd got the hang of it) was not to allow anything or anybody to disturb my current (and hopefully enduring) peaceful equilibrium, and to enjoy to the full all that providence had in store.

Our joint plan for the day – hatched apparently whilst I was having a nice little nap after swimming in the estuary (Alice's words, not mine) was to return to our favourite playground – Ramsgate Beach. As time was far too precious now to be waiting around for buses, it had been agreed that using a larger than average taxi was an indulgence worth making.

Bright sunshine was already visible from our floor to ceiling windows and the forecast was for temperatures to reach the mid-seventies by early afternoon. Discussing the weather had become almost as topical among the Australians as back home, as their concern at the lack of rain grew by the day. We sympathised of course, but not to the point where rain would be welcomed before our departure date in five days time. Until that day we aimed to soak up as much of the

God-given rays as we could, to show to our families the skin-deep evidence of having had a really good time.

As predicted, Lil arrived shortly after the rest of us had laid out our beach towels on the familiar patch of soft white sand. We'd been applying mild sunblock to the reachable areas of our bodies and utilising our neighbouring sister's hands to apply it to our backs. But all this activity came to a sudden halt as Lil came into view. Almost on cue the six of us lay down, some on their backs – eyes hidden behind the dark lenses of sunglasses, others on their stomachs – concealing their wakefulness. All were in fear of being coerced into activity before we were ready. Our fears turned out to be unfounded, and there was a collective sigh of relief, as Lil retrieved her own beach towel, sun block and book and settled down alongside us.

An hour or so later restlessness began to develop, prompting June – our queen of the waves – to take the first plunge into the crystal clear water, to cool off. The rest of us quickly followed. Keeping well within standing depth and using a rubber ball that Lil seemed to produce from thin air, we began to enjoy a game of catch. This was soon upgraded to a more competitive and organised game of 'forfeit', as Lil got into her stride doling out the simple rule – when you drop the ball you're out and a punishment will be levied at the end of the game by the winner.

Amongst peels of jeering laughter, I was the first to let the three-inch-diameter wet, rubber ball slip through my hand – banishing me from the game. Cautiously swimming out towards the shark net, I felt that this free time was the perfect opportunity for testing my reaction to deep water – now that I'd located the cause of the deep-rooted fear and hopefully exorcized the troublesome demon. But after stopping every

172

few yards to test the depth, as soon as the water became chin-deep, I was too nervous to go further. Disappointed, I swam back to base determined not to dwell on my cowardice and desperately hoping my forfeit didn't include deep water.

'Who's the winner?' I gasped after almost swallowing a mouthful of salt water when a wave caught me unaware.

'Who do you think?' mouthed Carol, cocking her thumb at Lil, who was moving along the line of obedient sisters handing out their punishments. Apart from my own – which was thankfully land-based – I can only remember one other forfeit: June was ordered to swim out to the shark net, and whilst holding onto it with one hand, use Lil's infamous whistle to play Waltzing Matilda, loud enough for us all to hear. It was carried out with ease and she was rewarded with a standing ovation from us all, along with my silent, envious admiration.

For my forfeit I had to ask the nearby café owner how long it would take me to walk to a place Lil had written down on a piece of paper, which, unknown to me at the time, was at least three hours drive away. He looked at me as if I was mentally retarded, much to the delight of my sisters. But this I could easily live with.

A game of beach cricket was just the thing for continuing the activities and the perfect way of drying off without soiling the beach towels. A piece of driftwood – strewn casually nearby – was utilised as a makeshift cricket bat, along with various personal items to mark out the wickets and other boundary points – that no one particularly adhered to. It was great fun getting into this sporting stride, with our neighbouring beach-lovers joining in the cheering and clapping each time a ball was hit well or a catch made.

Running in the soft sand to score points was hard work, but the encouragement of the growing crowds worked wonders on our leg muscles as well as massaging our egos.'

Whilst taking a break to quench our thirst, I noticed a woman walking towards us who looked vaguely familiar. Lil jumped up and ran to greet her, and as they stood talking, my memory released the information of who she was. It was Sheila; an old friend and work colleague of Lil's who I'd met on my previous visit. I was particularly pleased that she was to spend the afternoon with us because it gave me the chance to catch up and chat with someone other than a member of my own family. June was also pleased to have her on board, because it gave her a companion to share the often, lonely space of 'the smoker'. Her fun-loving personality guaranteed her immediate inclusion into an enlarged (albeit temporary) sisterhood of eight.

We were often told as kids that family was all-important and friends were unnecessary – especially in a family as large as ours. Although most of Mum's 'tellings' turned out to hold true, I could never bring myself to accept the second part of this one.

Lunchtime had passed us by while beach-cricket was in full swing, but our grumbling stomachs told us we'd need to eat soon, and as the RSL club was just a short distance away it was decided that this would be the most fitting place to eat.

After a hive of activity within the walls of the little toilet block, we emerged respectably sand-free, wearing clean shorts and tops. With four of us in each of the two cars – that were now available, thanks to Sheila – we headed for the club's car park.

On entering the cool, smart foyer of the club we were met by an equally cool, smart, young woman, whose facial expression reminded me of someone who'd just sucked on a sour lemon.

'Thongs are not allowed,' she broadcast, as she marched towards us with both her arms spread out in a gesture that was definitely not welcoming. Several of us automatically felt our backsides – to remind ourselves what type of knickers we were wearing – not yet thinking what business it was of hers. Lil 'to the fore' cleared up this confusion by telling the strident mare that no one was wearing thongs; we all wore clean sandals. A quick glance at our feet for confirmation didn't shut her up.

'Are you members? If not, I'm afraid you can't use the facilities of the club at this time of day.' We retreated back into the warm sunshine, as Lil moved forward into the clubs cool interior to deal with the politics of the situation.

Eventually she reappeared, having had her feathers well and truly ruffled by this uptight, unhappy female. 'I think we should take our custom elsewhere, I've met her type before, she's a real *jobs worth.*'

This development surprised us all, we'd been in the selfsame club many times eating, drinking, dancing and even playing bingo. But for some unknown reason, this woman had chosen to exercise her obvious power over our entry today, and what was even more surprising was Lil's failure to alter the woman's decision. Disappointment showed on every face except Lil's. This last visit to the club had been an important part of the planned pilgrimage – to revisit the area that held many memories for us all – and aside from all the emotional stuff, we were now absolutely starving.

Lil's feathers smoothed out as she once again took charge of the situation. Convincing us she was doing the best thing, we split into two groups and headed out to the Boat Club, having been promised better food, a much better view and service with a smile. Naturally she told Sheila where we were heading and was expecting her to follow in tandem, as there were apparently several ways you could drive to the Motor Boat Club – or was it the Sailing Boat Club?

'Is it far?' I asked Lil, as we manoeuvred out of the car park. I could tell she was still niggled, so I kept my voice affable though my stomach grumbled on.

'A ten minute drive - provided Sheila gets her arse in gear. Where the hell is she?' She continued to stare into her rear view mirror. The pun she'd just made wasn't brought to her attention, because within those words lay the simple fact that although her feathers appeared smooth and aligned, they were waiting to spring out like daggers at the slightest provocation.

What transpired over the next fifty minutes is so bizarre and unbelievable that you'd swear it was written for a comedy sketch to be shown on the big screen.

After driving out of the club car park we pulled into the curb to wait for the other car to emerge. It didn't. Not too perturbed at this stage, Lil muttered something about Sheila going the other way and set off on her own particular route, still keeping a constant lookout in her rear view mirror for the elusive car. We must have taken a few wrong turns and you didn't have to be particularly observant to notice that we'd passed through a certain junction at least twice, but apart from the odd nervous cough from the back seat we remained silent, knowing that it wasn't a good time to criticise, joke or even breathe too loudly.

After a much longer time than the promised ten minutes, we drove into the car park of the Motor Boat Club. No sign of Sheila and co. The usual rosy blush of Lil's cheeks had spread to cover her whole face, neck and ears, in spite of my effort at keeping the cars interior extra cool, by creatively handling the cars air con system.

'She should have been here ages ago, it's a simple enough drive,' raged Lil. No one commented except Alice. Her small, unemotional voice from the back seat suggested that maybe they were involved in an accident.

'Has anyone got their mobile?' I asked, knowing that they'd long since stopped carrying them everywhere due to the exorbitant cost of even sending a simple text message back to the Old Country.

'Sylvia's always got hers in her bag,' said the same small voice, then added unnecessarily, 'but she's in the other car.'

Lil snatched her bag from the back seat and rummaged amongst it's contents for her mobile, telling us between clenched teeth how she prided herself on never using her works mobile for anything other than work matters.

'But this is an emergency,' she added, feeling the need to square it with her conscience.

After what seemed like an age Sylvia's slow, relaxed 'Hello?' boomed through the little phone.

'Where are you?' snapped Lil, obviously relieved that they weren't crushed under a lorry, but not showing it in her voice.

'I don't know,' she replied in a painfully slow Lancashire droll.

'Well, ask Sheila or hand her the phone.'

Sheila's voice, though not as audible as Sylvia's, was clear enough. She relayed that after driving to the Motor Boat Club and waiting at least fifteen minutes for no one to arrive, she assumed we must have meant the Sailing Boat Club and that's where they were heading now.

'I clearly said the Motor Boat Club, Sheila,' Lil shouted over the noise of the car engine, as she backed out of the car

177

park, phone clamped between ear and shoulder. Suddenly backing over an unforeseen hump caused the car's passengers to grip tightly onto their seats and Lil's phone to flip from its secured position where it fell to the floor and cut the connection.

'Shit!' Lil said it, the rest of us thought it. I asked her with a hard-to-keep straight face, what was happening.

'Well, as they're so near the Sailing Boat Club, we'll head there.' She roared out of the car park in bottom gear, reminding me of the motorbike ride in the mountains.

As we crossed the familiar junction yet again, we saw Sheila's car cutting across a T road about forty yards ahead. Unfortunately they didn't see us. Lil ground to a halt, ignoring the loud hoot from behind and again punched Sylvia's number into her mobile.

'What's going on?' she demanded, almost taking a bite from the little phone. Sheila's voice came loud and clear.

'We're heading back to the bloody Motor Boat Club.'

Turning around, we proceeded again to the now, very familiar, junction. All sense of lane discipline and adherence to speed restrictions were completely ignored, as we raced down towards the finally chosen club. As we entered its car park, the other four were just piling out of their vehicle. With a look on her face that said, 'Woe betide any stroppy person who tries to stop me,' Lil ran ahead into the club's foyer, to sort out the formalities of entry.

Within ten minutes we were seated at a well located table overlooking the shimmering ocean. Lil disappeared to order a bottle of bubbly (I'm not sure if it was to celebrate our final arrival or to help realign her ruffled feathers). June and Sheila were puffing on cigarettes a discreet distance away, while the rest of us – thankful to be on stationary seats at last – sat quietly taking in the beautiful, tranquil surroundings.

As I watched Lil gradually unwind – thanks to the bubbly – I wondered what lay at the source of her core needs and which button had been pressed to trigger such behaviour. True enough, the sour-faced woman was a mean-spirited, authoritarian. But we'd all taken it for granted that she'd fall under Lil's usual charm. Perhaps Lil felt she'd let us down. Or maybe she thought *we* had let her down, for not supporting her effort to get beyond the bossy mare. Now wasn't the time to ask. A broad smile was back on her face and I wasn't going to be the one to make it disappear. Besides, I was newly pledged to hanging loose and going with the flow, and the flow, in the form of liquid bubbly, seemed to be having this desired effect on everyone.

My preoccupation with drinking the bubbly soon turned to thoughts of a stomach, longing to be filled. It was mid-afternoon and apart from our table, the club was almost empty, so thankfully there was no queue at the food counter.

Sylvia and I were the first to approach the blackboard displaying: Today's Specials. As we read aloud the dishes we might order, a burly, middle-aged woman appeared, with a large skillet in her hand and a look of thunder on her face.

'Chef's finished for the day and I'm here on my own,' she said, brandishing her skillet. I was far too ravenous to be intimidated. Sylvia turned to go, but I held her back and pointed out the sign that clearly read, 'Food Served All Day'. On the other side of the counter, the burly woman grabbed a large kitchen knife and sharpening steel then proceeded to attack one with the other. The look of thunder turned even blacker as she spat the words, 'I'll have to do it.' She then turned in the direction of the kitchen and hollered at the top of her almighty voice, 'I need help out here.' In spite of not being intimidated, Sylvia and I nearly jumped out of our skins. We placed our order and paid our money and in return we were given a small bleeper, with a curt instruction from the giver: 'When it bleeps come running.'

'Service with a smile! Wait till you see that old battleaxe back there.' This was Sylvia broadcasting in full volume. My suggestion that we have a quiet word (meaning out of Lil's earshot) with the others, about what to expect when they ordered their food.

Another round of drinks and relaxation descended once more. This was short-lived. A sudden buzzing movement at my elbow sent me running for my food amid a chorus of slow handclaps. The burly woman had thankfully mellowed a little. When she handed me the delicious looking food, she said sheepishly, 'It ain't easy being on your own. Enjoy your meal.' As I returned to the table two more buzzers could be heard, sending two more ladies frantically weaving through the tables, with bleepers held aloft.

To give credit where it was due, the burley woman did a wonderful job in satisfying our hunger and to give ourselves due credit, we told her so with words and a large tip. By late afternoon we discovered that she was in possession of quite a lovely face, when it melted into a smile.

The sun dipped slowly beneath the watery horizon leaving behind a sky vivid with colour – colour that was bounced back again and again from every reflective surface, and as we bathed in the rosy, cosy glow of it, a deeper relaxation descended on us all.

Had I been sitting next to Lil, this would have been the perfect opportunity to encourage an introspective conversation, to probe the recesses of her mind and find out what made her 'tick' in such a well-balanced way. Also to find out which emotional buttons had been pressed today, to put her in such an unaccustomed state.

George, having arrived straight from work ten minutes ago, to spend a couple of hours in our company and more importantly to satisfy his hunger, sat in the seat next to Lil. He chatted amiably about his day, whilst Lil sat, content to do all the listening.

All too soon the rosy glow cooled, and when harsh, artificial lights were switched on to compensate, the spell shattered completely.

Lil found her voice, spurred on by the need to continue some form of entertainment for her charges. Charades is no match for the natural entertainment of a glorious sunset and after trying extremely hard for half an hour, that too fizzled out like the rosy sun. Another half an hour or so was spent playing 'guess the singer of this song', before George heaved a heavy sigh and said 'time to go'. I asked Sheila if she had enjoyed her time with us and she replied simply 'It's been interesting.'

21

The ten thirty-five bus to Hurstville was late. But sitting
on the garden wall near the bus stop – in the early morning
sunshine, chatting merrily about the day ahead – took
precedence over the bus's arrival. That is, until we were told
by the owner of the garden wall that we were waiting in the
wrong place. Apparently this was where the bus stopped on
returning from Hurstville. Amongst a plethora of foul
language – aimed at the young receptionist (Miss 'Didn't you
know' who had given us this misinformation) we sprinted
around the corner just in time to see the late bus arriving.
We'd arranged to meet Lil in a café, close to the entrance of
Hurstville Shopping Centre and after yesterday's fiasco, we
were anxious not to be late.

She was already halfway through her skinny-latte when
we arrived at the rendezvous and she seemed completely
relaxed – which is contrary to what coffee does to me. After
ordering a pot of tea I joined her while the others – keen to
start shopping for the last of their remaining presents –
arranged to meet back at this very place for lunch, before
disappearing in a rush of excitement.

My most important task was to work out how many
Australian dollars I'd need to get me through our remaining
time. I hadn't exchanged all my money, because on my
previous visit I'd found it to be in my financial interest to
keep a watchful eye on the fluctuating money market and
exchange it appropriately. I didn't want to return to England
with surplus dollars, or feel the need to spend them
unnecessarily, so with pen and paper I calculated my needs,
whilst Lil read the morning news.

'Wow, I like that,' enthused June, as Carol brought out
yet another lovely top from her group of carrier bags, giving

a running commentary on which daughter it was for and how little it cost. This enthusing, admiring and rustling of carrier bags filled the corner of the rendezvous café, where we waited for our ordered lunches to arrive. All eyes fell on me expectantly. But I had nothing to show except a smaller than hoped for bundle of dollars. I explained that the two remaining presents on my list would be bought the next day in Sydney.

'Treat yourself to something, you miserable bugger,' cut in Sylvia, as she wrestled with a huge bra – trying to display it for us the right way up. The café was half empty, but all eyes settled on the pale pink, cavernous cups as it was held aloft for Alice to study the minutiae of its fastenings.

'You don't usually wear bras,' said Alice conversationally.

'I know I don't, so if it doesn't fit, I'll sell it to you,' replied Sylvia, equally conversationally, but four times louder.

'Why didn't you try it on before you bought it?' I asked, relieved that she'd finally shoved it back into its bag.

'I didn't have time to mess about, I had all this shopping to do,' and she held up two fistfuls of bags to prove her point. In spite of the poorer exchange rate and thoughts of an overloaded suitcase, I made up my mind to go with the flow and treat myself.

After lunch we again split into smaller groups, in order to fulfil our own personal agendas. I stuck with Lil, who was much less of a bad influence than the other spendthrifts. In fact she became the perfect, willing partner, in the purchase of my chosen treat, when we saw a fashion shop displaying the sign: Buy Two Get One Half Price.

Feeling content with my purchase and not wanting to be exposed to any more temptation, I accompanied Lil as she worked down her list of more mundane shopping chores.

'Where's Lil?' came June's conspiratorial voice from behind me, as I was idly watching the moving images of the news being broadcast on a public screen. I pointed to where she stood in the open-fronted bank foyer, halfway into the long queue of people waiting to be dealt with. June went on to say, in a lowered voice, that she'd seen something that might be suitable as a 'thank you gift' for Lil and George, but would like a second opinion.

After making an excuse to Lil, and arranging to meet up shortly, I followed June to a small tucked-away boutique where part of its space was given over to object d'art. She pointed out a pretty trinket box and matching photo frame – both studded with semi-precious stones.

'What do you think?' she asked, obviously pleased with her find.

'I've no doubt it would be well received June, but can you imagine it on display in their home?'

After pondering for a few seconds, and trying not to show her disappointment, she said, 'It's too fussy isn't it?'

'It might be for George, and the present is supposed to be for both of them, but I think photograph frames are a good idea.'

'I'll put the kettle on and make us a brew,' I said, opening the door of the motel room as Lil arranged the table and chairs outside – taking advantage of the late afternoon sun. By three o'clock we'd had enough of the busy centre, so we'd left the others still happily shopping and content to make their own way back.

As we sipped our tea, dunking a couple of the remaining ANZAC biscuits, Lil ran through the itinerary for the following day.

'Harbour cruise in the morning, Darling Harbour all afternoon. I'll be having my monthly meet-up and meal with my old work colleagues, but I've slotted in an hour at the end of the meal, for the rest of you to join us for a drink.'

I noticed that originally the end of the last sentence read – drinks, but the 's' was now almost obliterated under several lines of black ink. She continued to read out what she had planned as the grand-finale to the day – a pub crawl in the oldest region of Sydney.

'I was hoping to slot in a trip to the Museum and Art Gallery,' I said, waving a tourist pamphlet under her nose, 'I've still to get Barry's present and I feel the best chance for what I want is the Museum.'

'You can't just slot that in Marg, you'll need a whole morning and I can't see anyone else forgoing a harbour cruise for traipsing round a museum, can you?'

'No, but I've already experienced the harbour cruise, so I can spend the morning doing what I want and meet up at lunchtime for Darling Harbour.'

'I know you've been here before, but you don't know Sydney that well.'

'Here's a map, and I've a perfectly good tongue in my head,' I said reassuringly, waving another pamphlet under her nose.

'That's settled then, gotta go before the rush hour traffic builds up.'

'Thanks again, Lil for joining me with the bargain tops, I'll wear mine tomorrow.'

'I'll wear mine tonight, George is taking me to our favourite restaurant,' and she held it aloft to wave cheerio.

185

The other five piled out of the large taxi clutching a dozen or more bags between them. As I cleared the table – to lay out clean cups for the new arrivals – I could see that Lil was trapped at the end of the narrow corridor, as the mass of bodies and bags converged with sounds of excited chatter.

Refreshed from the several hours of doing nothing but drinking tea, having a bite to eat, and discussing the following day, we now felt ready to enjoy an evening out.

We'd come to learn that being Wednesday, it wasn't necessary to over dress, so we were ready in double quick time. Carol had made a lovely job of straightening my stubbornly-curly hair, after working her usual magic on Sylvia's.

Again it was a lovely, warm evening but in stark contrast to the meandering walk through the quiet suburbs of two nights ago, because we'd elected to be more adventurous and visit the untried, equidistant, Rugby Club, we now faced a straight, two-mile, down-hill walk along the busy, arterial road.

'Christ 'ow much further can it be, the bloke in the shop said it was just down there?' boomed out Sylvia, jabbing the air with a finger pointing in the general direction we'd been advised to go. Carol tried to lighten the situation by tuning into her usual rendition of 'Is This the Way to Amarillo?' But not having had a few drinks to relax and moisten her voice box, she soon fizzled out. Alice whined that her feet were starting to hurt and Sally whined back, in a parody of Alice's voice, that she should have worn shoes that were more sensible. Fifteen minutes later the sight of the club up ahead put a magical spurt into all our steps. Even Alice, I noticed, had stopped hobbling.

The Rugby Club wasn't very busy, but there were more people than expected and even more were piling in the door. We also noticed activity on the stage; suggesting something might be happening later. Alice thought it might be bingo and I thought, if it is, 'I'm going straight back home'. With this worrying thought circulating my head, I accosted one of the well-dressed club attendants and asked him what was happening.

My heart flipped with relief and joy when he smiled broadly and said, 'A very talented duo is about to entertain the pants off you.' I held onto this wonderful news long enough to secure a good table – with my seat facing the stage – then I instigated smiles all round by relaying our good fortune.

Within ten minutes the male and female entertainers filled the room with the music and words of a universally known song. We had bought a double round of drinks to satisfy our thirst from the long walk, and eyeing up the growing queue at the bar gave us all a smug, contented air, as we tapped our feet to the up tempo beat.

Several dancers were already moving around the space between our table and the stage. This gave us the opportunity – whilst downing our first drink – to give our individual opinions on: how old each couple was, whether we liked their mode of dress and most importantly, how much *we* rated their dancing skills – which on the whole, were very good. As panel judges we came to the joint conclusion that they were all members of a dancing school and this was a regular outing for them to hone their skills, or as Sylvia put it – to show off.

One man stood out against the rest, not head and shoulders, because he was very short – in fact, he was even shorter than us lot and as I've mentioned before we are all quite short. He moved with a graceful ease that was beautiful and compelling to watch. As he changed from one partner to the next – each one more than eager to take a turn with this short, middle-aged, bearded man – we decided that *he* must be the teacher of this so-called dancing school.

The second drink provided enough Dutch courage for us to take to the floor and dance in our usual fashion – grouped together, gyrating to the beat in an almost fixed position on the floor. Suddenly, the so-called dancing teacher walked boldly over to us and held out his hand ceremoniously to Sally, who, to our surprise, graciously accepted it. Off they went circuiting the floor like a couple of contestants in 'Come Dancing'. I'm sure she must have felt disappointed that she hadn't dressed up more, allowing her bling- bling to flash every time he twirled and swept her by the smiling, singing duo.

For a second or two we were struck dumb and immobilised. Then I leapt to the table to retrieve my camera, eager to record this unusual development and grateful that it wasn't me, because I would have tripped over his fast moving feet by now giving the rest of the gang the perfect opportunity to roar with laughter.

After the pair waltzed, quickstepped and jived through several songs with complete command of their movements, we started to wonder if it was a love-at-first sight thing. Sally had been single since her marriage break-up over thirty years ago, so technically she was available and it would be nice to have a really good dancer in the family, to add a little gentility to the important celebrations. Before the next song ended we almost had her married off. He returned her to us at the end of that song (maybe his hearing was as good as his dancing). He then held out his hand to June, who took it and took off, leaving us giggling into our drinks. Sally, flushed with pride, said that she'd thoroughly enjoyed the experience. Her words – spoken with a posh overtone – only added more impetus to our giggling causing her to fire back, 'You're just jealous, the lot of you.'

After several dances he released June and turned to Sylvia with his outstretched hand. For several seconds we all held our breath, anticipating a rush of Sylvia's verbal that would shatter the magical moment and embarrass the lot of us, including the short bearded dancer. But she too fell under his spell and as she reached out to take his offered arm to be led away, there was the sweetest of smiles on her face.

I started to feel very uneasy and it wasn't due to the fear of Sylvia embarrassing us, it had gradually dawned on me that he intended to dance with each one of us, and for some unknown reason, I didn't want to oblige. Disappearing into the ladies room to assess my options, I found June having a crafty smoke.

'Is he still dancing with Syl?' she asked, releasing a curl of smoke from her mouth.

'This is the third song, he deserves a medal,' I answered, before asking more seriously, 'I saw you chatting to him as you danced, what's he like?'

'His name's Graeme, he seems a nice guy and as you can see he's a brilliant dancer. But we were mainly talking about us; he was amazed that we were all sisters and how we were here visiting a seventh.'

After stubbing out the cigarette she opened the door to leave, and then stopped. 'I was nervous about dancing with him and making a fool of myself, but he's so good he made it seem effortless to follow his lead.'

Determined to ignore any more perverse fears and enjoy whatever came along, I returned from the ladies room and merged with my sisters on the dance floor. Sylvia was finally

189

being released after the fourth dance. With head held high, she slowly walked towards us, swinging her bottom and giving the impression of a catwalk model. On reaching us, this new persona was soon shattered. She poked me in the back and mischievously said, 'You're next.'

Feeling like a lamb being lead to slaughter I took his arm, thankful that my back was towards the several held cameras that were only too eager to capture my trepidation. I heard a single voice from behind call out, 'Relax and go with his flow.'

To my relief and amazement coordination developed between us. It felt so relaxing and enjoyable to be dancing with him that all thoughts of tripping and slipping just melted away.

Graeme wasn't good looking – as judged by our usual standards – but he manifested charm and confidence that went beyond the mere physical. Fortunately my memory released the appropriate steps of the three ballroom dances we twirled through. With him smiling through the light conversation, and me lost in a world of movement and music, I was only vaguely aware of the odd flash of a camera.

Carol followed me on the dance floor, all smiles as she was confidently led through a trio of more upbeat songs – causing me to wonder if Graeme had any input in which songs the duo sang.

Someone had to be last and on this occasion it was Alice. But unlike the fearful dread I'd suffered, her eagerness and happiness to embrace this experience was obvious. As Graeme led her away her eyes shone with delight, reminding me of how she'd looked while having the motorbike ride in the mountains.

190

'I'm not walking up that soddin' hill after all that dancing,' moaned Sylvia, well and truly back to her old self as she filled the now silent room with her Lancashire droll.

'A taxi's on its way,' said June patiently, as she proceeded to unfold a piece of paper showing two clubs where Graeme would be dancing over the next few days.

'But our last two nights are already planned and organised,' I said.

'I know that Marg, but how many things have gone to plan on this holiday? Besides he's such a nice man I felt bad about not taking this after he took the trouble to write it down.'

As we climbed into the taxi, I asked if anyone had found out if Graeme was a dancing instructor, but the tired looking, blank expressions, answered my question.

22

'We'll leave it up to you, Marg.' This answer had been given to me three times from three different sisters, after trying to get some feedback on the most suitable present for Lil and George. I'd fallen head first into a trap by announcing that I'd be spending the morning alone in the heart of Sydney, tracking down a suitable present for my husband.

The bus was just arriving to take us to Hurstville station where, accompanied by Lil, we would take the train to Sydney. I would disembark at Sydney Central, whilst everyone else continued on to Circular Quay. The day and evening ahead had been meticulously thought out. We each carried a bag large enough to hold a change of clothes as well as the usual: bottle of water, camera, sun block and make-up. The kitty purse had been transferred to June after being collectively replenished and there was a buzz of excitement about their harbour cruise, but my constant dripping – about the suitability of gifts – was starting to get on their nerves.

'Do you need some money up front?' asked Sylvia, taking her purse out of her bag and sighing impatiently.

'No, I've got enough money, I'm just concerned that none of you will see the present before I've bought it. What happens if you don't like my choice?'

'We, 'aven't got to like it, it's for Lil and George and you know their tastes better than any of us, and you've got the perfect opportunity to get it without Lil poking her nose in. So stop flappin' and get on that soddin' bus.'

Emerging from the gloom of the busy railway station into the brilliant sunlight of Sydney's business quarter brought me to a halt whilst I searched out my sunglasses.

A towering, kaleidoscopic scene stood before me. Architecturally impressive buildings housing massive sheets of glass reflected the moving, colourful images of cars, buses and people – all unaware of the beautiful, dramatic effect that was collectively created from where I stood. Unlike the laid-back atmosphere of beaches, clubs and tourist attractions that we'd become accustomed to, the cut and thrust of business and enterprise permeated the air. All around me smartly dressed people strode purposefully to their place of work. I consulted my pocket-sized map and strode just as purposefully in the direction I needed to go.

The Museum of Art was situated in the vicinity of a large area of parkland that contained an interesting collection of ancient trees and as I'd arrived ten minutes before its doors were due to open, I was more than happy to wander amongst these outdoor living sculptures.

A combination of clear morning air and the slanting position of the sun, gave a pure clarity to every detail of the large, convoluting trunks of the massive trees. I took several photographs of these visually irresistible subjects and then did something that was even more irresistible – I sat within one of the trunks. Even if I'd wanted to, the circumferences of these ancient trees were far too broad to perform any serious tree-hugging, so paradoxically I allowed the tree to hug me. Comfortable within its smooth, wood-fragrant interior, I sat watching the young park keepers busily working to maintain this lovely environment.

The sweet smell of freshly cut grass filled the air and on closing my eyes I was immediately transported back to my country home in England – a home that Barry and I had built with the help of a good architect and a small group of professional tradesmen; a home that included woodland, meadow and mature gardens, enhanced with ponds and sculptures that we'd created together over the eighteen years of living there. A home that in all probability we'd be leaving in the near future to embark on a new life on a volcanic island – where grass couldn't grow and trees, in the main, were palms or spiky cacti. Sentimental nostalgia washed over me as I huddled deeper into the tree's embrace. A quick glance at my watch forced my attention back to what lay ahead today.

One hour was allotted and spent in the vast area of the Museum of Art, which was barely enough time to even scratch the surface of the large amount of varied work exhibited. Within this hour I'd also managed to secure a tasteful pair of well-designed photograph frames from the Museum of Art's gift shop.

After a twenty minute power-walk down the broad, tree-lined avenues of state-owned buildings, I entered the Australian Museum and headed straight for the gift shop, aware that time was of the essence and buying this next gift was the main purpose of my visit. 'Surely you must have more stock for sale than this? I was hoping to buy an Australian fossil and was told by several sources that this was the best place,' I argued, finding it hard to keep the disappointment and frustration out of my voice – which was still slightly breathless from power-walking. The head sales assistant – who had politely greeted me on entering the museum shop, and guided me over to the mineral/fossil section – had already explained that stocks were low due to the low level of tourists at this time of year.

'Would you mind checking in your stock room?' I asked, not wanting to accept the inevitable.

'Certainly madam,' she said patiently and off she went leaving me to peruse the whole shop, because I was determined not to leave empty-handed.

I settled for a silk tie in rich colours of blue and gold with an aboriginal, white dot design, running across its surface. Not the preferred, elusive, native fossil, but a gift designed and made by native Australians (so I was assured). The rest of my short allotted time was spent wandering (or traipsing) through the contrived spaces that depicted Australia's near and distant past.

A nearby clock filled the air with melodious chimes, announcing that it was one o'clock. I was just a short walk away from Circular Quay where I could see a small crowd of familiar females clutching handfuls – of what turned out to be – cakes they'd secreted from the cruise boat. Lil was absent – apparently finding out the ferry times to Darling Harbour – so I used this opportune time to show them the photograph frames. Smiles all round was what I was looking for and smiles all round was what I got, and evidence of their approval of my choice came in the form of their portions of the cost being produced before Lil returned

Sydney Opera House was even more beautiful when viewed from the water on a midday harbour crossing. The golden glow of sunlight reflected off its tiled surface as it slowly receded – sandwiched between still blue skies and rippling blue water – allowing the onlooker the chance to appreciate the exquisite form of the whole building.

Sitting alongside us on the ferry were two females from New Zealand: Sadie – a Down's syndrome woman, and her mother. We struck up a conversation with this friendly pair, which developed into a delightful cabaret of fun as Sadie performed the 'Haka'. Apparently this ceremonial Maori war dance is only acceptable when carried out to perfection, with legs splayed out and slightly bent at the knees, hands on the hips and head pushed forward – allowing the intimidating effect of the whole length of ones tongue to be waggled ferociously. We fell about in fits of laughter as Lil tried her best to imitate Sadie's faultless performance and was then told – in no uncertain terms by Sadie – that she wasn't doing it right. To give Lil her due, she did make several attempts at this intimidating stance, which just created more laughter; whereas one blow of her whistle, would have demonstrated to Sadie just how easily intimidation can be brought to bear among the English.

The warm, open-hearted personality of Sadie touched us all, and we were all amazed to learn that she was forty-seven years old; because she didn't look a day over twenty-five. Several times she admired the pink bone necklace I was wearing and it gave me great pleasure to hand it over as a gift, as we neared the end of our short journey together. Sylvia's top had also been given a lot of attention from Sadie, but as this was the only thing covering her ample bosom, Sylvia diplomatically steered her on to a different subject. On reaching Darling Harbour we bade our farewells, thankful that we'd taken several snap shots of this pleasant little cameo of entertainment on our ferry across the water.

Food was now my immediate priority. I'd had nothing to eat since breakfast and the energetic walking around Sydney Central was beginning to take its toll. Cakes are no substitute for a nourishing lunch, and whilst I appreciated the spirit of the several offers made, all were refused in favour of my appetite for something more wholesome. So whilst the sights of Darling Harbour were indeed a feast to behold – compelling the majority of the gang to saunter along in awe –

with Lil at my side, we headed straight for the eating area to first, feast on the edible.

The relaxing afternoon spent at Darling Harbour had been thoroughly enjoyable. After eating a first class meal, several rolls of film must have been collectively used capturing the beautiful variety of fountains and contemporary water features that had been constructed in time for the opening of the Olympic Games in 2000.

Instead of returning to Circular Quay by ferry, we walked the longer distance through streets filled with shops. This inevitably led to more bags filled with shopping – in spite of the fact that we'd all supposedly completed our list of presents.

It was now early evening and Lil had gone to dine with her friends, where she was no doubt giving prior warning that her large brood of sisters would be popping by later to say hello and have a drink. We had also been given prior warning – not so much in words but by innuendo – that these were long-standing friends of hers, so best behaviour was called for. Bearing this in mind we commandeered the railway station toilets, to execute a complete makeover. Within two minutes the shelf behind the sink was filled to capacity with make-up, toiletries and hair essentials. We emerged twenty minutes later refreshed and revamped with sufficient confidence to meet the Queen of England.

'This one'll do, Christ I'm dying of thirst!' screeched Sylvia, as we were about to reject yet another almost empty bar in favour of one livelier. As we'd been given a definite time to arrive at the restaurant by Lil – as well as being shown twice where it was – we were now about to fill in a free slot of time with a much needed, thirst-quenching drink. I would have liked a nice cup of tea to be that thirst quenching drink – bearing in mind Lil's friends and best behaviour – but no, the bars were open and I was definitely outvoted, not by innuendo, but by broad Lancashire-accented words like: 'Sod off, I'm not drinking tea at this time of night.'

The atmosphere of Sydney Harbour subtly changed as the crowds of tourists disappeared with the setting sun and were replaced with city workers rushing to board whatever mode of transport took them home or just relaxing after their days toil in one of the many bars or restaurants.

Lil and friends were smiling expectantly as we joined them in the front line restaurant close to the station. We spent a pleasant hour of light conversation which naturally began with introductions all round. Lil's friends were six in number and this created a pleasant balance of one to one interaction However, each time a broad Lancashire dialect was heard speaking more than a few words all six of the friends turned in fascination to hear the spoken words, but not necessarily their content. We shared with them the high points of our holiday, cleverly steering the conversation away from the lowest points of the first few days; feigning memory loss whenever the words jet lag were mentioned. All in all I felt very proud to be one of the English sisters and very relieved (for Lil's sake) that no one had dropped any embarrassing clangers.

The streets of Old Sydney were quiet and dimly lit, and because the buildings here were mainly eighteenth and nineteenth century, it felt as though we could have been walking through any English town that had not yet been touched by the contemporary trappings of the twentieth century.

It was way past suppertime and although the consumption of food, as opposed to drink, was secondary to most of my sisters, we were all starting to get fed up and limp in the legs from lack of nourishment and too much walking. Lil had promised several times that the pub we were heading for was just a few more yards away, but we'd long since come to realise that like everything else in Australia, their yards were much larger than English ones.

'It's the oldest pub in Sydney and serves wonderful pie and mash,' Lil coaxed, oblivious to the negative memories these words evoked. I shot Sylvia a warning glance that she interpreted perfectly. It had been an almost trouble-free day and none of us wanted to be responsible for spoiling its last few hours.

The Lord Nelson was a quintessential English pub in every way – except for the balmy temperature of the air that you could breathe in without choking on tobacco-smoke and the Australian accents that pervaded every inch of its several bars. Heads turned as the invasion of English dialects rang out the list of refreshments when we finally reached our turn at the bar.

'What do you think of the food then?' asked Lil, knowing full well her question had been unnecessary. Apart from the sound of cutlery-in-use, lip-smacking and finger-sucking, there was silence until our plates were almost licked clean. The meat pies and puddings reminded us of our childhood days, when this quality of home-made food could be bought at any local bakers shop.

The childhood reminiscences continued long after the plates were cleared away. Carol laughed along with us as we recounted the good and the bad of the 'Old Days', even

199

though she was the only one amongst us that hadn't been around for most of that time; and the slight air of sadness about her made me wonder if she was feeling excluded.

I thought of the many times that I'd wished I'd been excluded from the consequences of belonging to such a large family, especially the embarrassing times at school when poverty prevented me from enjoying the every day things that my friends took for granted. It was in those early, teenage years that I'd made up my mind to fly the overcrowded nest as soon as I was old enough. I've never regretted leaving home when I did, but whenever these thoughts are given an airing they're always slightly tainted by the guilt and shame of the deserter. Thankfully my thoughts are my own and I had no desire to mar the happy-go-lucky ambience of this place and time.

Moving out of the Lord Nelson into the dark, starry night was like stepping back in time. This whole area – built by convicts over two hundred years earlier – took on an eerie atmosphere akin to Old London, during the time of Jack the Ripper. We instinctively huddled together, clutching our bags a little closer, as we stood waiting for the pre-ordered taxis. A coach and horses wouldn't have seemed out of place to transport us to the railway station. But the arrival of two sleek, modern cars immediately shattered this other-worldly illusion.

The last train to Hurstville looked filled to capacity with city revellers. However, after walking through several carriages, we managed to locate enough seats to enable us to stay fairly close together. Relieved to be seated and safely on our way back to our temporary home, we broke into a gentle sing-song in order to break up the uncomfortable silence of the carriage. Our fellow passengers seemed a little embarrassed to start with, but as the sing-song developed into our usual game of guess the singer and the year it became a hit, they began to join in the frivolity. Fifteen minutes into the journey and the whole carriage of people were singing their hearts out, and soon they were the ones calling for the next song, as soon as the previous one had been named and dated.

Amongst the passengers was a young woman who apparently worked for a local radio station. Her fascination at a bunch of women engaging the whole carriage in this way, prompted her to ring her place of work and hold her mobile phone aloft so that her colleagues could hear for themselves this unusual behaviour. Her fascination grew when she learned that we were seven sisters and she was about to start an impromptu interview, but the train was already slowing to enter Hurstville station. Reluctant to give up the opportunity of an interesting story she invited us to visit the radio station, but there was no time left in our holiday to accept her invitation.

As we stood to file out of the carriage the guy standing behind me confessed that he'd stayed two stops longer than he should have, in order to enjoy the fun. Clapping and cheering followed us off the train, plus one loud voice calling, 'You *pommie*-women can come and visit anytime.'

I walked with Lil to her car – mindful of the late hour and the dimly lit road where her car was parked. Meanwhile, my sisters waited a couple of streets away at the deserted taxi rank hoping against hope that this wasn't going to be a rerun of past endeavours. On returning, I told them that I'd seen a whole line of taxis parked just around the corner. Sylvia shot off in the direction I was pointing. Following at a slightly more leisurely pace – because by now we were dog-tired –

201

we turned the corner just in time to see Sylvia's panic-stricken face as she struggled to leave the back seat of the car she had just plonked herself into. With one leg on the pavement and the rest of her bulk still confined within the cars white body, we clearly heard her uttering a nervous apology. A mighty heave and she was running back towards us.

'They're bloody Police cars,' she blurted out, full of bravado now that we were out of earshot.

Within half an hour we had secured two legitimate taxis and were back at our motel.

23

The sudden sound of knocking on the motel room door was a welcome distraction from the weary job of trying to pack a suitcase that I knew would never hold the mountain of items before me. I opened the door to find June holding a dustbin sized, black, plastic bag, half filled with clothing and shoes. She bore the weight of it in both hands as she offered it up to me. 'I'm leaving this lot for Lil to take down the charity shop, do you want to look through them first?'

Prior to June's arrival, I'd been mournfully regretting every single item (other than presents) that I'd bought over the last three weeks. The headache and heartache of deciding what to leave behind in their place had now become the inevitable downside of buying them. But here I was, reaching for the black bag and peering inside to see what temptation lay among the neatly folded clothes.

June was made of stronger stuff. She refused to even look at the items that I'd half-heartedly started to relinquish, saying that her case was packed and not a single extra item could be squeezed inside. She had kept out her clothing for the evening and for travelling home, the former fitting neatly into her hand luggage. What she stood up in would be added to the contents of the black plastic bag.

'Come in and have a cup of tea, you deserve it,' I coaxed, impressed by her organisational skills and hoping a little would rub off on me. But she refused to step over the threshold into what she could clearly see was chaos.

The morning had started well. I'd woken early feeling bright and refreshed from a good nights sleep, and in the calm silence of early morning I'd composed a short poem to include in Lil and George's 'thank you' card. After breakfast Alice and Sally had left me in peace to sort out my packing and I in turn, would do the same for them when I'd finished. 'You've only got a fraction of the stuff we've got Marg, you'll be done in no time.' The memory of Sally's words as she'd walked out of the door was another reason contributing to my current state. The bright and refreshed feeling of earlier had now deserted me as I struggled mentally, physically and emotionally, to come to terms with what should and what could go into the suitcase.

Another knock on the door – gentler this time – produced a glimmer of hope that June might have changed her mind about the cup of tea. Carol stood on the threshold holding a large colourful carrier bag and wearing a smile as gentle as her knock.

'I can't come in,' she said apologetically, 'I just thought you might want to look through these clothes before I dump them on Lil.' Then she disappeared in a flash, leaving me holding the carrier bag in one hand, the open door in the other and a look on my face that would have been quite worrying to anyone who knew me well.

Determined not to bow to the temptation of ferreting through either of the bags, I placed them in the far corner of the room – out of direct eye contact – and went back to the task in hand. The mountain of items on the bed had diminished by approximately fifty per cent, but the suitcase was over three-quarters full, so I still needed to do more relinquishing and this was going to involve very careful consideration.

A third knock on the door in the space of twenty minutes nearly sent my frazzled nerves into total breakdown. A tirade of expletives, delivered at low volume through gritted teeth, accompanied the beach towel that was thrown across the room.

'Good morning, I'd love a cup of tea,' announced Lil's cheerful voice, as I swept back the door with more force than was necessary. Her eyes scanned the usually tidy room that now looked like a scene from Bedlam – without the noise.

'Maybe I'll be gaining a lot more than I thought,' she continued with a cheeky grin. She had obviously visited the other room first and been given the information that I was desperate for someone – anyone – to join me for a cup of tea. It was also obvious by the way her eyes continued to sweep the room, that she'd been given details of the two bags of relinquished fashion wear that had been left here, for first my, then her perusal.

I took the freshly made tea outside and sat at the small table; relieved to be away from the visual cause of my stress, even though I was mindful of the pressure to get on with the job.

'I see that I've gained another beach towel,' said Lil, nodding her head towards the crumpled heap of colourful towelling that was just visible from where she sat.

'No, I'm not leaving my beach towel behind,' I responded much too quickly, then went on to explain how it had cushioned my laid-out body on many a beach, both at home and abroad, and because of its quality still looked and felt as good as new.

The irksome subject of packing was thankfully changed to arrangements for the evening, and by the time I'd finished sipping the contents of my tea cup, a returning sense of calmness began to refresh my frazzled nerves.

'I haven't looked through these yet, I'm just hoping they don't contain anything that's too irresistible,' I said to Lil, feeling sufficiently composed to deal with the two bags of abandoned merchandise as I dropped them at her feet.

'Well let's find out then,' she grinned, as she took hold of the bottom of each bag and unceremoniously tipped the contents onto the floor, revealing two mounds of clothing of various colours and textures, interspersed with partially visible footwear.

For several minutes all thoughts of lack of space were forgotten as a jumble sale-like frenzy developed and dominated the pair of us. Words like: that's just your colour, fits like a glove and that's too good for the charity shop, didn't help my resolve. Lil had the luxury of time on her side, for deciding what she wanted to keep. A final compromise for me was a pair of cut-off trousers from June's bag and a black strappy top from Carol's. I would wear these items today and pack all my own clothes; except those for the evening and travelling. Hopefully by the end of today I'll have tired of these new acquisitions and leave them behind for Lil.

On returning to the impossible job of squeezing a quart into a pint size container, I decided to start thinking more laterally. Lil had left, taking with her the bags of unwanted items; to give me the space and peace to finish the task. It seemed that everything I wanted would just about squeeze into the case, provided I left out my beach towel – which by now I hated the sight of anyway – but there was a face-saving principal at stake, so I soldiered on. Due to its good quality, i.e. thickness, no matter how many different ways I rolled it or folded it, I couldn't accommodate the damn thing without removing an item equal to its bulk.

An extremely expensive, three-month-old pair of Italian leather boots – protected in their original box – was more or less equal to the size needed. I decided to travel home in these, instead of the designated comfortable, leather sandals that were several years old and after today could be dumped in the nearest dustbin.

As I sat on top of the bulging suitcase, bearing down all my body-weight in an effort to bring together the two component parts of the zipper, a loud rapping on the door and Sally's impatient voice filled the room.

'Come on Marg, how much longer are you gonna be?'

I jumped off the suitcase allowing its top to spring back and reveal the result of nearly three hours toil. Another impatient round of rapping began just as I reached the door.

'I'm not deaf,' I fired at the pair as they barged into the room and quickly closed the door as if old nick himself was after them.

'June's looking for someone to go with her to Hurstville and we haven't got the time to be waylaid any more,' burst out Sally, adding, 'haven't you finished yet?' when she spied my open suitcase.

'I just need someone's bum to sit on the case while I do it up,' I snapped.

'Well Alice's bum is bigger than mine, besides I'm bursting for the loo.'

Alice obliged, and after a few minutes of heavy sighs, two broken finger nails and a deluge of swear words, the suitcase was closed, locked and strapped. This brought on such an air of relief that I actually felt light-headed – or maybe this was just from bending over for too long.

'I can see you've finished then,' said June, as she joined me in the open doorway where I was endeavouring to bring normality back to my head via deep breathing.

'I'm popping into Hurstville for an hour, fancy coming along?' she asked, smiling expectantly. My honest response should have been that I had no intention of setting foot within a mile of any shops until after this trip was over. But what shamelessly poured out of my mouth without a moment's hesitation was, 'I think I've pulled a muscle in my back from manhandling that thing,' and I flicked my thumb in the direction of the innocent suitcase, then emphasised my lie by wincing as I bent to pick up Sally's discarded beach towel. 'I'm just going to rest up by the pool and hope I'll be fine by this evening.'

Although the late morning temperature was in the mid-seventies and the sky was devoid of clouds, due to the design of the motel, or the angle of the sun at this time of year, the pool and its fenced surround was almost in total shade. Carol was already at the poolside; her lone figure lying face down within the small patch of sunshine that crossed its far corner. She shifted to the far edge of this precious strip of sunlight, allowing me to squeeze in beside her and feel the relaxing warmth on my body – neither of us caring that I was wearing bra and knickers that didn't even match in colour.

Gradually we were joined by even more sisters, each one relieved to see the back of their packing and even more relieved to find more sunshine in the grassed area adjoining the swimming pool compound. June had returned from Hurstville looking despondent, but I shied away from discussing with her the reason for the trip and the subsequent futility of it. I was curious – given she'd already told me not a single item could be added to her baggage – but the lie of my bad back was proving difficult to live up to, so I kept my distance.

Fun and games began to develop when Alice brought out the blue and white crepe paper hats that she'd made earlier in the trip. Prior to today I'd have wondered, and voiced incredulously, why she'd kept them, but after the recent hours of anguishing over what I found difficult to discard, I thought it better to keep my wonderings to myself. As if reading my mind Alice announced to us all, 'Before packing the Rover's shirts and dumping these hats, (at this point she waved one of the tass005led efforts under my nose) we are all going to wear them one last time and perform the 'aka' as perfectly as Sadie.'

For most of my sisters, wearing the blue and white strip of their beloved team enhanced the performance that followed. Each gave their utmost to the ancient rite, unaware that several motel residents were gathering on their balconies to watch the spectacle and doubt the sanity of middle-aged, female pommies. When enough photographs had been captured on all seven cameras the paper, tasselled hats were unceremoniously dumped in the bin and the football shirts lovingly folded away.

By late afternoon all packing was out of the way and the more pleasant task of getting ready for our last night out was unfolding. After sharing a very late, takeaway lunch and loaded down with bags of discarded merchandise, Lil set off home to attend to her own pampering for the final fling with her sisters. Meanwhile Carol, booked solid as the family hairdresser, was turning their motel room into a makeshift salon; with a complete array of brushes, gels and sprays spread amongst the hairdryer and straighteners on the broad counter that swept along the length of the room. We were worked on in turn, without the slightest hint of complaint, at the time and effort given over to satisfying our vanity.

Dolled up to the nines for the last time on Australian soil, we boarded the two taxis and set off for Bankstown Sports Club. Lil and George would be arriving later with Sheila – who was happy to join us for our farewell night out, in spite of the recent, confusing escapade of the Motor Boat Club.

She was good company and we were more than happy to have her swell the sisterhood one more time.

It was approximately seven thirty when the taxis unloaded us at the entrance to what was obviously, a very popular and extremely well-funded club. As we walked into the high-ceilinged, spacious foyer, all eyes swivelled around the sheer luxury of its interior. Sensitively placed foliage, sounds of tinkling water and reflective polished marble; all combined to give the ambience of a five star hotel and the approaching gentleman that greeted us – dressed immaculately in the clubs distinctive uniform – completed the illusion. We were welcomed graciously and the preliminaries of signing in took no more than a minute or two.

After laying claim to a long table that bordered one side of the dancing area, and a good view of the band, I trotted off to find the clubs eating area; keen to stock up on edible energy before the night unfolded.

By the time Lil and George arrived with Sheila, the place was rapidly filling, so it was prudently decided (not by me) that a double round of drinks bought now, would save time later. Going on past experience I'd say – naturally to myself – that double rounds lead to double consumption by the end of the evening.

With drinks in front of us and everyone present, I passed the carefully wrapped thank-you gift to Lil along with the card, and with a toast from our first drink, we thanked her and George for all their help and support over the last three weeks. The gift was received in the spirit it was given and there was genuine good humour at the memory of the individual circumstances of each of the photographs displayed in their posh new frames. Alice, especially, was happy to see her blue and white tasselled hat immortalised atop George's broadly grinning face – even though it was a sad reminder of Blackburn Rover's defeat.

Cliff, the band leader, who happened to be a long standing friend and former work colleague of Lil's, joined us for a brief chat prior to filling the air with the throbbing, foot-stomping music that commanded everyone's attention. Within a very short space of time this Pied Piper of popular music had enticed most of his audience onto the dance floor, with the remainder happily watching the dancers, but unable to resist their own hands and feet from clapping or tapping to the beat.

It was a great night out and a wonderfully fitting end to our Australian trip. Sheila became the eighth sister once again as we danced the night away; topping up with fluid every now and then to keep us going. At one point Lil produced her Hawaiian-style garlands, which circumnavigated the heads of everyone on the whole dance floor before arriving back – miraculously without damage – into her possession. (To be used no doubt for welcoming the next batch of visitors to her adopted country).

The first ordered taxi to arrive was for Lil, George and Sheila, and as we were saying our goodbyes Sylvia came hobbling towards us complaining that she'd slipped and sprained her ankle in the ladies loo. Instead of the expected sympathy jeers and laughter rang out as one bright spark shouted, 'You shouldn't have peed on the floor!' and then another, 'You just want to get out of carrying your case tomorrow.'

Poor Sylvia, I'm sure she had slipped and twisted her ankle, but none of us were in the mood for negativity. Besides, you only had to look at Sylvia and you laughed; to look at her hobbling, made you want to laugh till you split your sides.

24

My eyes blinked open at seven o'clock precisely. There was no need to check the time, I'd long ago learnt the art of setting my inbuilt, mental alarm clock. And no matter how late it was when I retired, or how early the need to awake, the formula had never failed me – even after three weeks living in a topsy-turvy time zone.

Sally was also awake but still lying in her bed, no doubt focusing on the organisation of her time leading up to departing for the airport. I began to afford myself the luxury of reliving the enjoyment of the previous evening; tracing back from arriving here at twelve thirty and slipping exhausted into bed.

'Put the kettle on, Marg, I know you're awake,' Sally's hushed voice, cut into my reverie. I looked over to Alice who seemed to be still sleeping, or just refusing to open her eyes until she heard the welcome sound of the kettle being filled. I slipped out of bed, content to make my two older sisters an early morning cup of tea, aware that this would be my last chance of doing so for God knows how long.

As I waited for the kettle to give out it's usual singing hiss before clicking off, my eyes focused on the neat pile of clothing I'd set aside for travelling – which included a change of underwear and top – for when I arrived at Heathrow. But it was my choice of footwear that mainly held my attention and made me wonder, what had I been thinking? Travelling back in boots, considering the hot weather and the twenty-odd hours of cabin pressure of the long haul flight, was definitely a bad idea. My ancient, open-fronted sandals that were to be dumped today seemed a much more sensible option. And not for the first time, something told me that they'd be given yet another reprieve.

The soft leather of the calf-high, lace-up boots gave off the evocative smell of newness as I admired them once again. The sleek Italian design and the colour combination of red and black with a discreet white trim added to their desirability. And, on a more practical level, they were really comfortable. Sylvia had hinted more than once that if I was leaving them behind, she would gladly take them off my hands. I responded by telling her to go and take a running jump, then added, that she had less space than me, considering all the shopping she'd done.

'I'll soon make room for them by dumping a few pairs of knickers,' she'd replied with her usual cheeky grin.

What the hell, it's only a pair of boots. I scribbled a quick note, which read – 'enjoy them Syl,' and tucked it into the laces before nipping down to her door.

Barefooted and wearing only skimpy pyjamas, I tapped a melodious tattoo on their door, before leaving the boots outside and dashing back to make the tea. My reward for this act of generosity was Sylvia, knocking on our door five minutes later wearing a shortie-nightie, her newly acquired calf-high boots and a beaming smile. As she turned to head back to her room she flicked up her nightie using both hands, revealing her large, bare backside, as she skipped along the corridor. This thank you salute was performed without the slightest hint of a limp or a hobble.

Our organizational skills were honed to perfection as the juxtaposition of chores and ablutions – followed by breakfast in the motel dining room – ran like well-oiled clockwork. The only thing left to do was to get everyone's luggage down to reception, to await the arrival of Lil and George and two ordered taxis.

Sylvia's hobbling had predictably reappeared, causing a slight blip in our well planned schedule. Her sprained ankle of the previous evening had miraculously become a broken ankle today and every hobbling step was now accompanied with a painful looking wince, forcing June and Carol to take pity on her and carry her luggage. But no one was fooled; it just seemed more expedient to play along.

As we struggled down the wide, carpeted staircase we were treated once again to Sylvia's verbal description of how she had come by her terrible injury. Fits of laughter erupted from bodies already bent double under the strain of heavy cases, and one body up ahead, evidently couldn't take the strain because suddenly an extra large suitcase descended the stairs under its own gravitational pull. The site of it careering down, out of control, but landing neatly at the bottom – none the worse for its unaccompanied journey – created yet another burst of the giggles. In the event, apart from the embarrassing noise, this proved to be the easiest way of transporting the biggest cases down to ground level – especially as these were owned by the two oldest sisters and a younger one who was purported to be disabled.

Sydney Airport, as expected, was teeming with people both leaving and arriving the vibrant, sun-soaked country that had become our home for the past three weeks. We each loaded our luggage onto individual trolleys with the help of Lil and George, who then went to secure a large table in one of the cafés, for a farewell cuppa after we'd checked in.

All was going to plan when suddenly Sally's voice rang out from the front of the checking in queue. 'How much?' she broadcast, more as a belligerent statement than a question. And, although it was aimed at the airport attendant just a few inches in front of her, everyone in the queue – in fact everyone in the terminal – could hear and all eyes now focused their attention on the incident. Sally had been singled out for a very hefty, excess baggage charge, even though Alice – standing in the queue next to her – had just sailed through with a case larger and heavier. Unfortunately, she couldn't spread that surplus weight onto any of her sisters; we were all up to, or over, the weight limit ourselves. She was in no frame of mind to do what Alice did at Heathrow – become the bag lady of Sydney Airport – so there was no alternative but to pay up.

Alice and I handed over the remainder of our Aussie dollars to help take the sting out of the fine. Sally was reluctant to accept the money – stubbornness and independence is a family trait – but after we were just as stubborn with insistence, she accepted the help graciously. Thanks to the attendant serving that particular check-in queue, Sally's persecution complex of three weeks ago had returned.

Lil and George were tucking into rolls filled with egg and bacon that were needed (according to George) to overcome their hangovers. George was very upbeat considering he had a hangover, laughing out loud when we told him of Sally's misfortune. I put this down to over-excitement at the thought of having his life and his wife back into a normal routine, without the infringement of her six sisters. But as we left them at the entrance to the departure lounge, his demeanour changed and I'm sure he too, felt genuine emotion as we all hugged and thanked them both for their tireless support throughout our trip. I felt especially sad saying goodbye to Lil, knowing it would probably be at least two years before I could share the company of my best female friend.

216

The following twenty four hours were a reverse sequence of the journey out three weeks earlier. The first leg of this return journey to Hong Kong – again on a half-empty flight – meant there was space enough to spread out and sleep. But as we were all bright eyed and bushy tailed, this was unnecessary. So in order to fill the first few hours of travel, the in-house entertainment screens were put to full use and I decided to catch up on some reading – a book I had to start again from scratch – to refresh the distant memory.

Relaxing, classical music accompanied us as we wandered like zombies around the almost empty terminal of Hong Kong airport. It was a relatively short stop, allowing the cabin staff to thoroughly clean the interior of the plane, while refuelling and checks were done on the exterior. We had been advised to take all our hand luggage with us and this was piled onto the two trolleys that were helping to support our tired bodies.

We were in sleep mode and this quiet, restful place was a perfect opportunity to obey our physical demands. Several street wise passengers had found themselves a row of empty, upholstered seats to use as a makeshift bed; knowing full well it may be their only chance of lying down for the rest of their long journey.

We had opted once again to refresh ourselves by splashing cold water on our faces in the ladies room and then proceeded to wander in and out of the many shops selling all manner of desirables, except the thing we desired most, a cup of tea. At one point I suggested having a little nap, but I was outvoted by all manner of excuses that boiled down to one thing – fear of the plane taking off without us. I could have taken advantage of this fear, knowing there were plenty of hands to shake me awake at boarding time, but as we'd agreed to take turns pushing the trolleys, I felt obliged to remain upright.

Safely back in our allotted seats we found a completely different scenario to when we left them. The plane was now packed to the gills with people, and like three weeks ago, a hefty proportion of these people were families with children. Added to this discomfort was the very cold temperature of the air conditioning, which the cabin crew seemed reluctant to alter, despite the repeated moans and groans of the mainly English passengers.

Cabin blankets and pillows were at a premium, but we sisters had never been shy about asking for what was ours by right, and if warmth couldn't be supplied via the vents, then other means would have to suffice. All bound up in fleece blankets, complimentary socks and eye pads, we resembled a row of misshapen chrysalises about to emerge into – well the mind boggles at the thought. But how we looked came secondary to how we felt, the determination to feel warm and get a little shut-eye was far more important.

Surprisingly enough, I managed to procure some quality sleep. Maybe the cool temperatures had helped, although it hadn't stopped several of my sisters from emerging out of their cocoons in frustration at not being able to visit the land of nod, and instead watched films or played computer games.

I was starving by the time breakfast came rattling down the isle. Although my watch was displaying 5.00a.m. English time, my stomach – still influenced by the southern hemisphere – was demanding its main meal of the day. This welcome diversion from the monotonous hours of sitting in a fixed position lifted the spirits of all my fellow passengers, bringing on a buzz of excited anticipation into the slightly warmer air. Even the members of my own family, who hadn't managed to get any sleep, found their customary sense of humour bursting forth at the smell of food.

Mindful of my four hour-ride to Devon by bus, and the strong demands my stomach may well make, I concealed several items of food and drink into my hand luggage and hoped that it wouldn't be noticed as I passed through customs. I knew full well how sensitive officials were about transferring foodstuffs from one country to another. But I salved my conscience by telling it that these items were all individually seal-wrapped and I'm sure, contained enough chemicals to deter any prospective bug from immigrating to England.

25

A beautiful May-day morning greeted us as we touched
down onto one of the many runways of Heathrow Airport. It
was six thirty precisely – the time of arrival that was printed
on our tickets. This feat of perfect time keeping, in an
industry fraught with uncertainties, filled me with awe and
respect. But these positive feelings began to falter when the
frustratingly slow pace of extricating ourselves from the
plane took its toll on our patience.

We had arrived at terminal three; but Alice, Sally, Sylvia
and Carol needed to get to terminal one for their connecting
flight to Manchester – with less than an hour to spare. And
the uncertainty of how long we would have to wait for our
luggage, added to a mounting sense of panic. June and I had
plenty of time for boarding our respective buses – which
were conveniently located at terminal three – but were
anxious to see our sisters meet their destined connections.
So, after grabbing our luggage from the carousel we all shot
off on an obstacle course of moving floors and turning
corners, in the direction of terminal one.

For the first time, I experienced the vastness of Heathrow
Airport and how fit you needed to be (both mentally and
physically) to get from one terminal to another in a hurry,
whilst keeping your mind focused on the confusing array of
directions.

Sylvia bemoaned her ankle several times, but gave
up when nobody took the slightest notice, let alone gave her
any sympathy. June and Carol, who had done most of the
heavy lifting of cases onto individual trolleys, kept a
watchful eye for bags toppling from there precarious perches,
as we scurried along the twists and turns. Sally, who was
way ahead of us most of the time, took on the role of most
panicked, continually checking her watch and looking back

at us, frustrated that we weren't moving as fast as her. For my part, I did what came naturally – keeping a concentrated eye on all the signs leading to where we needed to be – calling out, left or right when a change of direction was necessary. Alice, well, she just took it all in her slow, steady stride, which meant she dropped behind several times, causing one or other of us to wait for her to catch up. She couldn't or wouldn't be rushed and that's all there was to it.

Of course, we made it in time – the alternative was unthinkable – although it must have passed through everyone's minds (except maybe Alice's). And now it was time to say our hasty goodbyes. They were so eager now to get back to the bosom of their families; and the need of a good nights sleep was evident in their drawn faces as they tried to be bright and cheerful. Coupled with the natural sadness of parting, I felt a deep sense of disappointment in myself, for not having made the most of the three week opportunity to show them how much they meant to me. I hugged each of them in turn and tried my best to impart in that hug all that I'd denied them in words. A few days of jetlag would interfere with the memory of the experiences we'd shared, but hopefully, when those few days passed, they would all be remembered and appreciated.

After retracing our steps to terminal three at a more leisurely pace, June and I headed for a welcome cup of tea and an even more welcome wash and change of clothes.

Feeling more refreshed we made our way to the bus terminal with a half hour to spare before my bus was due to leave. The two of us chatted amiably about nothing in particular, but beneath the surface each was aware of the imminent sadness that parting would bring, and equally aware that neither of us would express that sadness verbally. My determination to hold her close and tell her how much I was going to miss her was scuppered when she winced in pain the moment I wrapped my arms around her.

'What's wrong?' I asked, concern taking precedence over everything else.

'It's nothing,' she said with a heavy sigh, 'I must have strained a muscle in my chest from all the heavy lifting.'

The obvious pain she was suffering, coupled with her total lack of sleep during the past twenty-four hours, added to the air of sadness about her. Words failed me even now and my impotence to help make things better for her, weighed heavily. After gingerly holding her close and promising to meet up very soon, I watched her walk away to board her bus, knowing that like me, tears filled her eyes and sorrow filled her heart.

After twenty minutes of time-consuming manoeuvres through the airport one-way system and the stop-start of a maze of traffic lights, the bus gradually picked up speed. The steady drone of the engine filled the silence of the almost empty bus. My book, which was to help pass the long hours ahead, remained closed on the vacant seat beside me.

June was still on my mind, causing a mixture of concern and intrigue. The concern was for her health and happiness – which to me, have always been inextricably linked. And, if I was to be completely honest, the happy-go-lucky June of old seemed to have been partially hidden behind a veil of sadness, for longer than the last three weeks. The intrigue was at her strong desire to move back to Lancashire, after living on the beautiful island of Jersey for over thirty years.

She had made no secret of the fact that now her three sons were grown up and independent, there was a gaping hole in her life that she felt could be better filled in her hometown

where most of her siblings still lived. Although the larger
family would no doubt welcome her back to the old
hometown with open-arms, several of us wondered at the
wisdom of her strong desire. For my part, I'd learned the
lesson: 'you can never go back' many years ago.

*During 1966, after spending my first six months working
away from home, I returned to find that I couldn't settle back
into a lifestyle that I'd happily outgrown. Within a month I'd
left permanently, to share a house with two girl friends in
London. The sad, hurt look on Dad's face when I'd said,
'there's nothing here for me now, Dad,' could still be
conjured up in my mind's eye accompanied by that lingering,
corrosive sense of guilt.*

*And whilst on the subject of guilt – out of the three of us
that had left home, I was the only one to have deliberately
and conscientiously dumped my Lancashire dialect, after
applying for the enticing position of telephonist/receptionist.
This London-based job was only available to young women
who spoke without the encumbrance of a strong accent.
Instead of taking the option of a different job – and those
were plentiful in the 1960's – I worked hard to eradicate
what was then classed as – stigmatised communication. It
wasn't difficult to achieve; being away from my old friends
and family helped, but having a strong desire to accomplish
it helped even more.*

*The last few years of my life at home hadn't been
particularly happy, and to my mind, the downturn started
with a move from a large council house that was surrounded
by gardens and wild countryside. Whilst living in this house I
clearly recall the many happy days spent playing on the
nearby sand hills that overlooked the beautiful River Ribble.
I remembered the walks through Bluebell Woods as we*

223

trekked to Darwen Tower – a doorstep line of young
children, each clutching their lunch of banana-buts and a
bottle of tap water, supplemented with a handful of
raspberries, blackberries or anything else that was edible
and growing on route along the arduous, but immensely
satisfying journey. They were happy, carefree, innocent
years.

But the years that followed – although punctuated with
some high points, were mainly spent beneath a dark cloud of
despair. I struggled to come to terms with a move to a part of
town, filled with back-to-back, terraced houses, no gardens
and not a single tree to soften the harsh horizon of smoking,
factory chimneys. My perceived worsening standards of
home-life – made even more difficult with the arrival of two
more babies – prompted my determination to escape, just as
soon as I was old enough. In the meantime I spent any spare
time alone, walking on the moors or hitch hiking to the Lake
District and sometimes just sitting in the cemetery; at least
there were flowers and greenery here. Thinking back, the
easiest option of escape was to wait until I was old enough to
marry. Instead I'd opted to caste my net into the wider
world in the hope of securing a better quality of life,
unaware that a thread of guilt was inextricably woven into
that net.

I wondered now if June's desire to return to her home
town was fuelled by a similar, subconscious guilt trip, or
maybe I was just reading too much into a situation that bore
no resemblance at all, to my own.

A long time ago I heard a little parable that I found very
profound and very helpful whilst dealing with a difficult
situation. The situation has long been forgotten, but the
wisdom contained in the parable has stayed with me.

Two men were walking down opposite sides of the same road. As a car passed between them one man shouted to the other, 'Wasn't that a lovely red car?'

'Yes it was a lovely car, but you were mistaken on the colour, it was black not red,' answered the other man, and an argument developed about who was right.

Alongside this same road grew a strong, tall tree, where a third man sat perched amongst its highest branches. He had also seen the car pass by beneath him and it had in fact been red on one side and black on the other. Both men were right, but only from their limited view point whereas he had the advantage of being elevated above that limited view point and could see the whole truth of the situation.

Pondering now on the simple truth contained in that parable filled me with humility. June knew well enough what was necessary for her happiness and my arrogant surmising wouldn't make the slightest difference to anything. But I did regret not making more of an effort to encourage her to discuss the subject whilst the opportunity existed. My eyes closed and I concentrated on the gentle, rocking movement of the bus, hoping to gradually still my thoughts and stop the useless worrying about things that had passed.

Whack!!! I couldn't tell if it was the sound or the pain of hitting my head against the window that suddenly jolted me from a dream. I'd been climbing a tree and one of the branches had given way, causing my arms to flail about as I fell. At the same time the bus had turned into a motorway service station and driven over a particularly high speed ramp – violently jerking my sleeping head and leaving me completely confused. Embarrassed, I looked around, but

225

fortunately no one seemed aware of, or interested in, my sudden entry into wakefulness. Their full attention was given over to the driver and whether they could leave the bus for refreshments.

'I'm only stopping to pick up a colleague,' announced the overweight man as he proceeded to deftly remove his large backside from the incongruously small driver's seat. 'I'll wait ten minutes for anyone wanting to buy a drink,' he added after seeing the change in their beseeching faces turn sour and menacing. Within thirty seconds I had the bus to myself.

This particular bus, although comfortably modern and equipped with toilet, was surprisingly devoid of refreshments. So with great satisfaction and self congratulation I opened the bag of goodies that I'd snaffled from the plane. The bag's contents had been added to by most of my sisters – eager to prevent me from looking half-starved when Barry met me at the bus station in Exeter. For a minute or two I thought about sharing the cache with my fellow passengers when they returned. But it turned out that most of the weight and space in the bag was taken up by the packaging of each morsel, and before anyone returned to witness it, I'd eaten the lot. A small bottle of water and my book was all that remained to accompany me the rest of the way.

As the bus rolled over the county line into Devon, I felt the usual thrill of the home run that greeted me after every spell away from home – but today that feeling was heightened. The splendour of this glorious county, on this lovely May day morning was breathtakingly beautiful. Paraded before me, at an average speed of sixty miles per hour, was the changing landscape through towns, villages and countryside; all decked out in the finery of trees and shrubs dripping with blossom. From the grandeur of manor houses to rows of tiny cottages, all became equal in status as the impartiality of Mother Nature blessed there surroundings with colourful, new growth.

The glimpse of a man tending his vegetable patch accompanied by a little girl, reminded me once again of the only house I'd lived in as a child; where there was a garden large enough to grow any vegetables. Dad had been so proud as he held before the whole family a small heap of new potatoes that had taken weeks of painstaking care to produce. We'd never stopped teasing him about the small reward after so much effort, but this hadn't deterred him from repeating that effort time and again.

I seem to be the only member of our extra large family to have developed a similar passion for gardening, which means that I am the only one to experience at first hand, the joy and satisfaction that Dad had felt: a satisfaction that comes from delving into the warm, late summer soil to retrieve the fruits of a labour that was never begrudged, no matter how small the harvest, because satisfying a need to help things grow is reward enough. My kitchen garden has provided Barry and I with all our fruit, vegetables and herbs for the last seventeen years. I have Dad to thank for sowing the original seed.

Agitation filtered through my fellow passengers as we neared our destination. It was a gorgeous day and they were anxious to be released from the stuffy confines of the bus. But I was feeling particularly refreshed and chilled out. I'm sure the earlier sleep had helped but I was also aware of a slight 'shift' deep inside.

With eyes closed, I brought into focus each and every member of 'my family'. They were all held in my heart, and most were still there at the end of a telephone or a car journey – even Lil, living at the other side of the globe, was only a day away. For years I'd felt that I'd deserted them, when in reality I was just doing what felt right at that time.

A lot of my early decisions were made without much conscious thought, but there always seemed to be a hidden force nudging me in the right direction. Maybe it was time to put more trust in that force and accept what the future held. What was most important now was planning the list of the planting that was necessary when I got home. My trip to Australia was over; it was time to pull my finger out and catch up with all the overdue jobs in the garden.

THE END